Did Not Finish

NICOLA MARSH

Stranded…with my nemesis!

AXEL: It's bad enough an unseasonal blizzard means I'm stuck with my PA's annoying cat, but to make matters worse, Mia Samson and her poison pen are in my house too. The renowned reviewer has tanked enough books with her dreaded DNF and I need to teach her a lesson.

But my enemy is not what I expect and if I'm not careful, I'm in danger of revealing my secret to the one person who can use it against me.

MIA: I know people in publishing call me the career-wrecker behind my back. What they don't know is, I'm writing a novel, and when I'm lucky enough to win a week-long retreat with bestselling Axel Low in quaint Sugar Plain, Nebraska, I'm thrilled.

Until I discover being snowed in with the reclusive grump is merely the first trope my life has turned into, and soon I'm sorely tempted to enact enemies to lovers…

Which one of us will lose the plot first?

Chapter One

MIA

"I have a severe case of blue balls."

I roll my eyes at Jace, my co-worker, who thinks the proximity of our desks in the editorial department of the New York Press equates with a close friendship worthy of him divulging every snippet of his sex life.

"I have no interest in the color of your gonads," I say, trying to focus on my latest review for a debut author's psychological thriller. I love my job, and that so many of the newspaper's readers hang on my every word for their book choices, but it's times like this, when I'm trying to find the words to say 'this sucks' politely, that it's tough.

"My balls aren't literally blue, Mia." Jace, who channels the quintessential bad boy in every romance I've ever read with his artfully mussed hair, laconic smile and perpetual stubble, leans back in his chair and smirks at me. "I thought you of all people would understand sexual frustration."

I shouldn't bite, I really shouldn't, but the faster I get him to shut up, the sooner I can return to the task at hand: trying not to ruin a new author's career while being honest and maintaining my credibility.

"What's that supposed to mean?"

"When's the last time you had a date, Me-me?"

He knows I hate it when he calls me that, but I pretend it doesn't bother me. Either that or fling my stapler at his big head.

"I've been swiping right plenty," I say.

It's a lie. I deleted my dating apps months ago after a spectacularly bad coffee catch-up with a guy who wanted to play footsies under the table while licking the foam off his cappuccino suggestively. Ugh.

Jace eyes me with understandable doubt. He knows that when he calls me late at night with a last-minute invitation to join him at an impromptu poetry reading at some grungy bar I'll go, which means I rarely have a date.

"Cobwebs form when something isn't used in a while." He holds up his hands in mock surrender. "That's all I'm going to say on the matter."

The stapler might do some actual damage if I throw it at him and I can't afford to lose this job, so I settle for flinging a pencil. My sporting prowess is on a par with my dating skills, so I miss him by a foot.

He tsk-tsks and smirks, so I ignore him and return to coming up with the right words to not decimate a debut author's crappy book.

Shows promise. Lie.

Clever red herrings. Lie.

Looking forward to the sequel. Lie.

Nobody knows why I'm so pedantic with my reviews these days. Why I spend an inordinate amount of time choosing my words carefully. Why I proofread my reviews way too many times.

Because one day soon, I hope I'll be on the receiving end, and I want reviewers to be kind.

Yeah, after five years of getting paid to read and review books by the best newspaper in the city, I'm writing a book.

It's a big deal for me and I haven't told a soul because I have enough doubt demons perched on my shoulders whispering how utterly crazy I am without actual people I know sharing their skepticism. Or worse, laughing at me. And they will. The romance genre may be the biggest seller worldwide, but it constantly cops unfair criticism from ignorant people who might get a pleasant surprise if they actually picked up a romance and read it.

And what I'm writing, a regency romance, is particularly disparaged with the stupid 'bodice ripper' moniker. Though with a little luck, by the time mine's published, the popularity of Bridgerton will pave the way for me to make my mark in the sub-genre.

I can dream, right?

I'm also tinkering with a suspense novel, an idea that keeps intruding whenever I try to write the regency, and I've written the first three chapters. I've plotted the rest of the novel because every night when I try to sleep, the story unfolds like scenes from a movie playing behind my eyelids. I take it as a good sign. I can't wait to dive back into the manuscript. That's the beauty of being a newbie writer. I can follow my muse wherever it takes me.

And I'm hoping it takes me to Sugar Plain to spend a week with Axel Low, America's number one crime bestseller.

Entering the competition to win a seven-day retreat alongside five other writers with the most popular author in the country is a long shot but I had to try. His books are incredible, and I have no problem finding words to describe them in my reviews: taut, edge of your seat, compulsive, page-turners. He's my hero and to have him mentor me for a week would take my suspense manuscript to the next level. I'll happily shelve my regency romance for now and focus on my crime writing skills if I get firsthand feedback from a writer of Axel's caliber.

In this industry, it's all about networking. So if I'm lucky enough to meet him in person, it's not just the writing tips and critiques that will be invaluable, but he'll know people—agents, editors, publishers—who I'll need in the future if I want to go down the traditional publishing route.

And that's my ultimate dream: to walk into a bookstore and see my baby on shelves. To pick it up in my hands, weighing it carefully, caressing the cover, before flipping it open and inhaling.

Is there any better smell than that of a new book?

"What are you thinking about?" Jace's aim is better than mine and his eraser bounces off my arm. "You've got this dreamy look on your face. Maybe you're getting some after all?"

"Leave me alone. I'm working." I muster my best disapproving frown but predictably, it has little effect on Jace, who's oblivious unless whatever we discuss revolves around him.

"Bull. You're daydreaming about some hot guy." He places his elbows on his messy desk and rests his chin in his hands. "Tell me now, because you know I'll get it out of you eventually."

He won't. I'm not telling a soul I'm writing two books at once in the hope of getting published. Especially not Jace, who would tease me mercilessly.

"Okay, you got me. I was thinking about the hero in this romcom I read last night." I fan my face. "To die for."

"Speaking of romance, have you read the latest Adele Lavash novel?" He wolf-whistles. "Man, does that woman have a way with words to get you going."

I roll my eyes. "She's a hack, churning out the latest in erotica to make a quick buck."

A lot of bucks, considering her books consistently top the bestseller lists. A mega successful indie author who keeps her identity secret, I've read every one of her books: and left scathing reviews for them all. Though technically, saying I've read them may be a stretch. Skimmed, more like it, because they're so repetitive.

Her prose is average and the plot minimal. Nonstop sexy times does not a novel make. Though I hadn't intended on causing such a furor with my last review. A lot of readers had piled on my disparaging comments, rehashing my review on a popular book lover site, and it hadn't been pretty. I half expected to get an abusive email from the author, considering there had been considerable fallout and that book hadn't sold nearly as well as her others, but thankfully, she's a pro.

Did I feel bad for labelling her last novel DNF? A little, but my reading time is so precious that if a book doesn't grab me and I put it aside, I'm honest in giving it a Did Not Finish in my review. I couldn't even be bothered skimming that one, it had been that bad, and I tried to be objective.

It's not like I don't appreciate a scintillating reverse harem tale, I do, but the last Lavash novel had been lacking in key areas like conflict and it had been a disaster. The book's rankings backed me up, but I do have a conscience and I can't help but imagine how I'll feel if the same happens to me.

"If you ask me, when you're in a dating drought like you are, maybe reading about sex might shake things up?" Jace snaps his fingers. "Maybe you should download Lavash's entire backlist and glom to your heart's content over the weekend?" He winks. "Get you in the mood, so to speak."

"You're a pain the ass," I mutter, and hoist my PC screen higher so he can't see my face. "I'm working here. You should try it some time."

"Getting some will fix that bad mood too, you know," he says, and my frown is useless when he can't see it.

Besides, I know what will improve my mood.

Winning one of those coveted spots on Axel Low's writing retreat.

My review quotes have helped boost authors' careers over the years and if there are literary gods, I deserve some good luck karma.

Chapter Two

AXEL

It's the bane of my existence that my publisher and agent are based in New York City. Not that I regularly make the trip from Sugar Plain to Manhattan, but the culture shock is real every time I leave Nebraska. The teeming sidewalks are the worst. People are rude. They bump and jostle and glare, always in a hurry to be somewhere. Give me the wide-open spaces any day.

Considering my dourness, I fit right in here. Most would take one look at my formidable expression and go out of their way to avoid me. But I have a reason to be grumpy. What's their excuse?

I enter the cavernous café, a converted warehouse with exposed steel beams, brick walls and rough-hewn wood, and spot Christine sitting at a corner table with her nose predictably buried in a book. I like that about her, that she doesn't just read her clients' manuscripts or wannabe author submissions all the time, she also reads for pleasure. We have that in common.

At fifty-eight and two decades older than me, Christine Foley is an icon in the publishing industry. She gets deals done. It's not uncommon for her to get her authors six or seven figure advances regularly. She's the queen of auctions. She's my heroine.

And the only person in publishing who knows my secret.

I'd like to keep it that way, which is why I'm here. For the sales of my upcoming release to surpass that of my last, she insists it's time I reveal my face to the world and that means hosting a writing retreat for aspiring authors.

It's the last thing I feel like doing.

I value my privacy. Not for me, per se, but to protect the one person in the world I'm doing all this for.

But Christine assures me that getting the six participants to sign ironclad non-disclosure agreements will ensure my privacy remains intact. I'm not so sure. I don't trust easily, never have, and that means I'll be keeping a very close eye on the writers who've apparently 'given their left nut' according to Christine to spend a week with me.

As I wend my way between the tables, I wonder how Christine hasn't aged in the ten years since she first signed me. Sleek black bob, minimal wrinkles, and fire-engine red lipstick, her signature. Only the spectacles are different, her current choice of small round lenses and thin tortoiseshell wire rims giving off a distinct Harry Potter vibe.

When I reach the table, she looks up, a frown between her brows at the disruption, and I smile. I get the same look, part-confusion, part-annoyance when I'm interrupted mid-paragraph.

"Axel." She stands and envelops me in a cinnamon-scented hug. "It's so good to see you."

"You too, Chrissie."

When we sit, my gaze lands on the book she's reading, the latest Colleen Hoover blockbuster.

"That's a good one," I say, pointing to it. "She has a way of dragging you into the story from the first page and never letting go."

Christine nods and shoves the book into her bag. "She's my guilty pleasure."

"Why guilty?"

"Because I feel guilty for reading her when I should be finding an author exactly like her I can rep."

I feign being wounded by pressing a fist to my chest. "But you've got me. Are you saying I'm not enough?"

She waves away my false modesty. "You're more than enough. Now tell me, are you ready for this retreat?"

I grimace and shake my head. "I'll never be ready, but I trust you, and if you think this is necessary to boost my sales, I'll do it."

Her eyebrows draw together and her gaze flits around the café for a moment, her uncertainty worrying me. "The industry is in flux so whatever we can do to sure up your next contract, I think it's worth doing."

My concern intensifies. I know I can reinvent myself at any time in indie publishing, but the comfort of a large advance goes a long way to alleviate my insomnia when I pace my den at night, worrying about what will happen to Paula if I can't pay the bills at the exclusive care facility where she's thriving.

I shift in my chair and clear my throat. "The industry's always in flux, so what aren't you telling me?"

Her nose crinkles and she can't quite meet my eyes. "It's all about social media these days and many of the publishers' big sellers are going gangbusters after achieving viral status online."

She doesn't need to spell it out. I have minimal social media presence and in these days of voyeurism, where everyone wants to see what everyone else is doing, that makes me increasingly irrelevant. Sure, I have my super fans who buy anything I publish, but with the proliferation of indie publishing, I know I'm not grabbing the new readers who may not have heard of me. Promotion-wise, I have a virtual assistant I pay handsomely to send out newsletters and organize paid advertising, but I don't post selfies or photos of my desk or do book signings.

That's a major bugbear with my publisher too, the 'no in-person events' stipulated in my contracts. I can't have curious eyes delving into my personal life. Paula deserves better than that. But in this age of over-sharing online, I understand why this is becoming more of a problem with the sales and marketing team who figures out how much to pay me for my advances.

"What you're saying is, if I can take a few photos of my protégés slaving over their works in progress during the retreat, it'll be a good thing?"

She nods. "Absolutely. Have you chosen the winners yet?"

Yeah, but I wonder if those writers will think they've won anything when they spend a week with me. I'm an organic writer whose words come from nowhere and pour onto the page when I put my ass in a chair. I treat writing as a job, not something to be done whenever inspiration strikes, and I know my opinion isn't popular with many creative types.

"From the twenty my PA shortlisted, six were definite standouts."

"Good, that should make it easier on you if the competition winners have a modicum of talent." She pauses and slides her glasses off her nose. "Your assistant has taken care of all the indemnity stuff?"

My best buddy Cole—Buzz to me because I swear he gives himself a fresh buzz cut daily—was a lawyer in a previous life so I trust him when he says the NDA and indemnity insurance are solid.

"He's done everything, from all the legal stuff to the accommodation to ensuring the pantry and fridge are well-stocked."

"What about alcohol?"

"We're going to be writing for seven days, not partying for a week."

At least, that's my plan, to give the winners cursory feedback on their partials, then hide out in my den or library for the rest of the time, avoiding social contact as much as possible. I can't think of anything worse than spending time with a bunch of gushing writers intent on picking my brain.

My jaw tightens as I mutter, "Definitely no partying."

Chrissie barks out a laugh. "Trust me. When you're holed up with six writers who'll be hanging on your every word, expecting you to impart great wisdom to take them from slush pile to bestseller list, you'll need a drink."

I join in her laughter but it's only for show.

I'm not looking forward to this writing retreat one bit.

Chapter Three

MIA

"Tell me you're not taking his entire backlist." My best friend Rosie, perched on the end of my bed and sipping champagne while criticizing my packing skills, points at my overflowing suitcase.

"Okay then, I won't tell you." I try to squeeze an extra pair of sneakers into the suitcase, but it doesn't work. Not surprising when I've packed twenty books, two pairs of jeans, one skirt, a maxi dress, three tops, a spare jacket, thermals, and underwear. It's obvious where my priorities lie.

"You'll look like a suck-up if you ask him to autograph all those." Rosie tut-tuts. "You want to make an impression with your writing, not give the great Axel Low an opportunity to label you a stalker."

I survey my suitcase that has no hope of zipping. Rosie may have a point. I do want to make a good impression, and I hoped showing Axel I'm a huge fangirl might help. But lugging many thrillers he's written all the way to Nebraska may not be my brightest idea. I have no intention of paying the airline extra if I'm over the weight limit, which is more than likely with all these books, and once I land in Omaha I have to board a train for a two hour journey to Sugar Plain and don't want to lug a heavy case around. Besides, the weather channel is predicting an unseasonal snowstorm, so I'd be smarter replacing a few books with winter jackets.

"I still can't believe you're a chosen one," Rosie says, raising her glass to me. "*The* Axel Lowe picked you as one of his protégés for a week. How cool is that?"

Beyond cool. So cool I can scarcely believe it. Because I haven't told anyone apart from Rosie that I'm writing—and I only told her after I won a coveted spot at the retreat—I have no idea if I'm any good or not. I contemplated joining a local creative writing group who meet monthly at the local library and critique, but that would out me if someone recognized my name and I'm not ready. The last thing I need is some author I've given a poor review to learning that I'm writing and disparaging me online, ensuring I lose my credibility at the paper.

I'd also contemplated submitting my work to a group of beta readers online, or hiring a freelance editor, but the manuscript isn't finished yet and when I do seek feedback, I want them to have the whole picture.

An excuse born of fear? Maybe. But thankfully, I don't have to worry, as Axel Low chose me as one of the winners for his retreat and that gives me some of the validation I crave.

I've been so hyped over the last week while waiting to hear about my entry that I've reread the first three chapters a thousand times, tweaking words, editing sentences, making changes until I was cross-eyed. When the email landed that I'd been one of the six chosen, I'd celebrated by ordering way too many upcoming releases online, adding to my towering to-be-read pile because being surrounded by books centers me.

Being chosen means I must have some modicum of talent according to one of the fiction writers I admire most and spending a week under the watchful eye of Alex Low will open doors for me I never dreamed possible.

Rosie snaps her fingers in front of my face. "You're envisaging your name on a book cover, aren't you?"

I swat her hand away. "Ssh. Don't jinx it."

"What's to jinx? Thanks to the tutelage of Axel Low, my best friend is about to become a revered novelist." She sips her champagne and smacks her lips. "Whose book will be made into a movie, and I'll get to ride on her coattails at the red-carpet premier." She winks. "Not that I'm thinking too far ahead."

My pulse races at the thought of being published let alone any of that other stuff Rosie mentioned. "You're making me nervous."

"Don't be, you deserve this." Her smile is understanding as she raises her glass again. "You're a winner, babe, whatever happens."

I pick up my untouched champagne flute and tap it gently against Rosie's. "I don't think it's sunk in yet, that he actually chose me."

"Believe it, baby." Rosie downs the rest of her champagne in two gulps and wiggles her eyebrows. "Do you think he's hot?"

"He could look like a troll, and I wouldn't care. I'm there for his literary expertise, remember?"

Though I have to admit, I am curious, particularly when I can't garner his age online. Many authors publish under pseudonyms but it's rare to have a prolific bestseller with minimal online presence. It's frustrating, because the more I know about Axel Low, the more I can use that information to my advantage and wow him.

Rosie, who's single and not loving it, rolls her eyes. "It doesn't hurt to have something nice to look at while you're slaving over your manuscript."

"True, but it's his mind I'm interested in."

I picture Axel Low as a Stephen King type: distinguished, powerful, awe-inspiring. I'm hoping I can string coherent words together when we talk so I don't come across as a bumbling idiot.

"Well, whatever the mysterious Axel Low looks like, don't forget to put in a good word for me."

Rosie knows nothing I say will sway Axel to use her PR services. She's a whizz with online influencers and has run several successful book tours for lesser name authors, but the advances Axel commands means his publisher's publicist takes care of his marketing and Rosie doesn't stand a chance.

"I'll talk you up on one condition."

"Anything."

"When my first book's published, you'll tout me at a discount rate."

Her eyes shimmer with sentimentality. "Baby, you can't afford me, but I'll think about it."

We laugh and top up our glasses, pausing to clink again before downing half our champagne.

Bubbles make Rosie giggly and she's grinning when she gives me side-eye. "How's Jace?"

Rosie's the picture of innocence with her big brown eyes and guileless expression, but I know better. She's been dropping Jace into casual conversation on a regular basis for a few weeks now, ever since they met at my impromptu birthday drinks after work.

I'd already warned Rosie not to go near Jace—being privy to

his extensive dating history daily means I know his moves too well—and I issued a similar warning to Jace about not toying with my best friend. But I'd seen them together that night, faking disinterest while casting surreptitious glances at each other, and I know my warnings may have acted to fuel their curiosity.

After that night, Jace had asked me about Rosie, but I'd cut him down and he hasn't tried since. Rosie has no such compunction.

I waggle my finger at her like a disapproving aunt. "Jace is a serial womanizer and you're too good for him."

Rosie snickers. "Let me guess. He uses dating apps like the rest of the planet except you, so that makes him a womanizer."

"Nothing wrong with dating apps." Except when I use them and discover my brunch date is decades older than his profile pic or my drinks date used a pic of a wannabe actor to lure me in. "But there's dating and there's *dating*."

"So Jace has an active sex life." Rosie winks. "Means he's experienced and that can't be a bad thing."

Mutinous, I compress my lips together, but she tickles me, and I end up laughing. "I'm not giving you his number."

Her eyes sparkle with mischief. "I know where he works, Cupid. If I want to contact him, I could."

"So why haven't you?"

She contemplates my question for a moment, her head tilted to one side. "Is that a challenge?"

"Hell no."

For a moment, my bubbly friend is pensive. "Honestly? I don't want you caught in the middle of anything if it gets messy."

Knowing Jace, it's bound to, and I'm relieved. "That's sweet."

"It's also delusional, because I'm letting my loyalty to you interfere with my love life."

"Trust me, sweetie, there's no love with Jace involved."

"Lust is better anyway." She raises her flute again. "To me, finding a guy my bestie will approve of. And to you, having the time of your life with Axel Low."

I shake my head but must admit I'm curious about the secretive bestselling author and can't wait to meet him.

Chapter Four

AXEL

I watch a snowplow clear the road leading to my house. When I first heard the weather forecast of unseasonal snow in late fall, I hoped we might get a blizzard and I'd be snowed in, unreachable by the six writers who want to pick my brain for the next week. But while the dump has been impressive, it's not enough to cut me off from the world and I'm expecting five of them to arrive tomorrow.

Mia Samson, however, is arriving today.

I made sure of it.

I have a lot to say to Miss Samson.

Book reviewers are a major part of my job and I'm eternally grateful to anyone who takes the time to read and review my books. But Ms. Samson's reviews in the New York Press are particularly influential and it's time she knows exactly how powerful words can be.

It irks, that her submission was good enough to catch my eye, so while I may have initially selected her for this retreat to teach her a lesson, I can't help but wonder if she really has talent or those first three chapters I read were a fluke.

It wasn't the plot that grabbed my attention—there are a lot of diabolical sister stories in crime fiction—as much as the writing. A snappy style bordering on irreverent, with a hefty dose of tongue-in-cheek thrown in. Not many suspense novelists have that flair and I'm curious to see how much of that manuscript she's completed.

The rest of the winning partials have varying degrees of talent, but none stood out as much as Mia's, and I found myself rereading it late last night, sucked into the story all over again. It's rough and needs work, but if it's her first attempt at writing suspense, I'm jealous. The first novel I penned is firmly buried in a document folder on an old computer and will never see the light of day. Filled with clichés and unlikeable characters, I'd shelved it after paying an exorbitant sum to a freelance editor who'd given damning feedback along the lines of *'this manuscript is riddled with problems from the first chapter to the last and would require a significant rewrite to be readable, so I suggest you set it aside and work on something new.'*

I wanted to throw my computer against the wall after that, but I hadn't. I'd spent the next six months reading a lot of suspense novels in the genre I was targeting and got a feel for the market. I also completed five online masterclasses by some of the bestselling authors I could only aspire to be like, and then I started writing again. My first manuscript, the 'riddled with problems' one, took me nine months to write. My second, that would ultimately earn me representation from Christine and a big advance at auction, took me four.

I submitted the first three chapters and synopsis to twenty agents. Five sent generic rejections within a week, two asked to read the full manuscript—one of them being Christine Foley —and she'd called me two days later, raving about how much she loved my story and outlining her vision for it. My publishing career had snowballed from there and most days I still feel like it can be ripped out from under me because readers will realize I'm a fraud.

Not a fraud, exactly, but someone who's used to having life upended and is expecting another derailment at any time.

Heavy footsteps clomp into the living room, and I turn to see Buzz pulling a beanie onto his shaved head. "Mia Samson's due to arrive in ninety minutes so I'll head into town and pick her up. Anything else you need while I'm there?"

"No, all good."

"Is it?"

Buzz's steely gaze bores into me like it's done from the time we met in the hospital five years ago. His sister had been a passenger in the car accident that left Paula with an acquired brain injury, and we'd spent a lot of time together pacing the waiting room. We had a lot in common: both loners with no family bar our sisters, and reluctant to talk about our pasts. As we bided our time, praying our sisters would wake from their comas, I had to do something proactive, so I'd found a place for Paula and me to live far from Atlantic City.

I'd pulled up a map of the country on my cell and stabbed a finger at it, landing in Sugar Plain, Nebraska. I bought this sprawling ranch in the middle of nowhere for one reason: it had a driveway that ran for a mile and I could see whoever was driving up. No way would I let her stalker ex blindside us again; when he got out of prison, that is.

But Paula never got to move in with me, no matter how much I wanted to look after her. I was willing to hire private nurses around the clock, but the doctor convinced me how much better off she'd be in a facility with trained professionals. I wanted Paula to have excellent care and the doc advised that Sunny Pines had a stellar reputation but exorbitant fees that precluded most people from being accepted. Luckily, I'd instigated measures to be able to afford the fees, because my sister deserved the best.

At least Paula had woken up. Sadly, Buzz had to make the decision to turn off the life support machine for Sue, his sister, but in a way, I envied him that closure. To see my vibrant, bubbly sister go through what she has…it's been torture.

"From where I'm standing, you don't look so good at all." Buzz gestures at the six makeshift desks set up around the cavernous living room. "Why are you letting these strangers into your life?"

"It's business. You know if I had a choice, I wouldn't do it."

Buzz runs a hand along the back of his neck, his go-to gesture when he's seriously pondering something. He's a man of few words so when he speaks, I've learned to listen. He eyeballs me with blatant skepticism. "We always have a choice."

If only that were true. If I had a choice, I wouldn't be churning out five books a year. I wouldn't be chained to my desk. I wouldn't be hiding behind a pseudonym to protect Paula. And I sure as hell wouldn't be spending the next seven days with aspiring writers.

Buzz assured me the non-disclosure agreements they signed are ironclad, but I don't trust people. All it takes is one leak of my real identity, and my whereabouts, and Paula will suffer.

I won't tolerate it.

But I'm doing this for Paula. To ensure her care is ongoing. One more mega advance should do it and that means giving the publisher what they want: publicity.

The attendees have been worded up; no pun intended. They can tweet and reel and video as much as they want. In fact, it's encouraged, as long as my face and the exterior of my house isn't in any of them. The last thing I need is Paula's ex doing a reverse photo search online and discovering where I live.

Buzz's glower is formidable. "You sure about this, boss?"

Buzz knows I hate it when he calls me this. Technically, it's true, he works for me, but we're buddies rather than boss and employee. He's been my confidante since the accident. Our friendship had sprung from a horror but these days I'm not sure what I'd do without him.

I give a brief nod. "I'm sure."

Buzz's heavy sigh indicates he sees right through my lie because I'm not sure about anything these days, least of all opening a part of me long guarded.

But it must be done.

Paula deserves the best, considering I'm the reason she ended up in that accident and her life is ruined.

Chapter Five

MIA

I'm a city girl. Born and bred New Yorker, so while I can appreciate a weekend escape in the country, the moment I step off the train in Sugar Plain I feel like I've entered an alternate universe.

There's quaint, then there's *quaint*, and this town looks too picture perfect to be true. Or maybe that's because I'm a *Gilmore Girls* fanatic and always pictured myself living in Stars Hollow—complete with my very own Luke, of course— but as I pull my wheelie suitcase and leave the station, I can't help but gawk. From the gazebo in the middle of a grassy town square dusted in snowflakes to the red-brick shopfronts decorated with flowerpots, the diner on the corner to the cutest bookshop I've ever seen, Sugar Plain is definitely channeling Stars Hollow and I can't wait to explore.

But I'm being picked up and taken directly to Axel's place so my exploration will have to wait. I haven't been given an itinerary of the next seven days but I'm hoping to have some free time. I can't imagine being chained to a keyboard for that long. Which is ironic, because I am for work, but this is different. Writing is my creative outlet and I need to give my muse space to breathe. She's fickle and doesn't appreciate being told to perform on command.

A newish black pickup truck rumbles to a stop not far from me and a giant of a man unfolds himself from behind the steering wheel. He's huge, at least six-four, with a buzzcut, thick black beard, and shoulders that could heft a bookcase or two. He's wearing jeans and a flannel shirt, without a jacket despite the freezing temperature, giving off a distinct lumberjack vibe as he ambles toward me.

"Mia Samson?" His voice matches the rest of him, deep and commanding, and I nod.

"That's me."

"Cole Williams." He sticks out his hand. "But my friends call me Buzz."

I'm not sure what to call him so I shake his hand and smile. "Nice to meet you."

"I'm Axel's personal assistant and housekeeper so if there's anything you need during your stay, don't hesitate to ask."

I struggle to hide my surprise. This guy looks like a local farmer, and I can't imagine him running an author's business and household.

He must see my skepticism because the corners of his mouth twitch with amusement. "It looks like you won't be convinced of my excellent housekeeping skills until I whip up one of my signature apple pies. I'm famous for them around here."

"Can't wait," I say, embarrassed that he can read me so easily. "Is it far to Axel's place?"

"About ninety minutes." He eyes my single suitcase and raises an eyebrow. "That your luggage?"

"You were expecting more?"

He shrugs. "Guess I thought a writer would bring two cases for books alone."

I laugh. "Is that what Axel does?"

A shadow passes over his face. "Axel doesn't travel much." He hoists my suitcase. "We better go."

I'm not sure if he's uncomfortable talking about his boss or if I've hit a nerve, but I'm determined to find out a little more about Axel before I meet him. An hour and a half drive is plenty of time to do some subtle probing for information, even if Cole seems reluctant to chat.

Like any good groupie, I've researched Axel Low thoroughly, but there's not much about him online apart from the generic: brief bio that states he's loved reading since he was a kid, enjoyed English at school, eschewed college to work, tinkers with cars for a hobby. The rest of his bio lists how many books he's had published over the last ten years—forty —how many copies he's sold worldwide—thirty-million—and how many languages he's been translated into—twenty-nine. Impressive figures, especially the copies sold, and if I can be one-tenth as successful, I'll be happy.

I hoist myself into the passenger seat after Cole stows my suitcase in the pickup tray. It's comfy and considering I didn't sleep well last night—fangirl nerves—I hope I don't nod off.

When he gets behind the wheel, I ask, "Do you have to pick up everyone attending the retreat?"

"Yes, but the rest don't arrive until tomorrow."

That's weird. Not that I think Axel's a psychopath luring unsuspecting writers to his lair, but I realize I'll be on my own tonight in a place I don't know with two men who are strangers. The perfect way to start one of Axel's thriller plots and I hope he's not prone to doing firsthand research.

The engine rumbles to life and Cole glances over his shoulder before pulling out onto the road. "Don't worry.

Axel's a stand-up guy, your bedroom door has a lock, and I have my own cottage not far from the main house."

Once again, Cole's read my mind, but he hasn't really assuaged my doubts. It doesn't make sense, me arriving a day early, and that's when it hits me.

This could be a golden opportunity.

Rather than envisaging Axel to be an axe-wielding murderer with nefarious motives, I should take advantage of some one-on-one time with a world-famous crime author.

How many writers would give anything to be in my position? Countless, so I need to shelve my overactive imagination and focus on making the most of the next twenty-four hours before the rest of the competition winners arrive.

"From the research I've done, Axel's a private person. I'm surprised he's allowing us into his home and didn't book somewhere else for this retreat. I mean, non-disclosure agreements are well and good, but still."

Cole doesn't take his eyes off the road, but his fingers flex a little against the steering wheel, gripping it tighter, like my question has made him uncomfortable. "He prefers to work at home, especially when he's on deadline."

I don't ask the obvious, 'he's on deadline yet allowing a bunch of strangers into his home for a week?' Cole seems reluctant to talk about Axel and I doubt he'll tell me much anyway. His loyalty to his boss is admirable but I wish I could find out some useful snippet before I arrive.

"Have you been his PA and housekeeper long?"

"About five years." He casts me a quick glance that's more a formidable glare before refocusing on the road. "He's a good guy."

I don't need the reassurance but it's nice to hear. Before I can ask anything else, Cole turns up the radio. Surprisingly, it's a smooth hits station—he seems more of a country and western kind of guy—and the volume is loud enough to discourage further conversation.

Hint taken, I lean my head against the window, admiring the snow-covered fields and watching flakes fall from the sky. It's beautiful and I feel like I'm in fairyland. Complete with a secretive prince who holds the keys to the publishing castle.

I hope he's not a toad.

Chapter Six

AXEL

The snow's coming down hard when I spot Buzz's pickup wending its way up my long drive. It rarely snows here late-fall, and the last time Sugar Plain had a blizzard that cut off the town had been eighty years ago. That'd be just my luck, to be marooned here with a bunch of strangers. But my obsessive checking of the weather forecast assures me this freak snowstorm will pass quickly and I hope the meteorologists are right.

It's times like this I wish Paula was closer, but the best special accommodation for acquired brain injury patients happens to be in Connecticut so I don't get to see her often enough. I try to chat with her twice a week but when I'm on deadline that can stretch out to once every two weeks. The sad thing is, she doesn't seem to notice.

It guts me to see her sometimes, especially when she's having a bad day. The doctors advised me at the start that she'd have long-term cognitive deficits—slow responses, lack of concentration, difficulty understanding speech, poor short-term memory—and some days she exhibits all of these. Not to mention her physical problems: dizziness, loss of balance, headaches, visual disturbances, chronic pain. It breaks my heart to see her suffer, a potent reminder it's my fault she's in that place, unable to care for herself let alone use her brilliant mathematical skills to teach the way she once had.

Buzz pulls up in the carport and I crane my neck to get a glimpse of the illustrious Mia Samson, she of the poison pen. Mia appears suitably smug in her social media profiles, often seen with a pretzel in one hand, a notebook in the other. She's pretty in an understated way, with shoulder-length strawberry blonde hair, big green eyes, and a wide smile, but all I see when I look at her is the enemy.

Dramatic? Maybe. But that woman is messing with my career, and I won't stand for it. Paula receiving the best ongoing care is too important for anyone to screw that up, least of all some wannabe writer who gets off on tearing down other people's work.

I can't see much of her as she steps down from the truck. Jeans, white sneakers, a black long-sleeved jersey that improbably skims her midriff and exposes a flash of skin as she stretches, and a vibrant emerald scarf. She must be freezing. Impractical as well as narrow-minded.

Buzz takes her around the back as instructed to get her settled. I'll meet her soon enough. Too soon, for my liking.

I glance around the living room, pleased with the set-up. The fire's roaring, there's a designated space for a charcuterie board on the coffee table, and the six makeshift desks have neatly stacked notebooks, pens, and index cards. With the low-slung caramel suede sofas near the fire—my go-to reading spot —reading lamps on handcrafted wooden tables beside the sofas, and large cushions strewn on the floor for those who prefer to sprawl, it's a writer's paradise.

It has to be, because the more photos the writers take of

the environment, the less likely they are to hassle me.

I know they'll ask questions about my reclusive life. I'm prepared for it. But I invent stories for a living, so I have my responses prepped. The last thing I need is loose lips flapping my secrets despite the non-disclosure agreement.

I hear Buzz clomping through the kitchen before he pauses in the doorway to the living room.

"She's here," he says, unnecessarily. "Getting settled in her room."

"Thanks. Any problems?"

Buzz eyeballs me because he knows what I'm really asking: 'what's she like? Is she going to drive me nuts?'

"Seems nice enough. Knows when to keep quiet." His mouth kicks up into a semi-grin. "I admire that."

"As a man of few words, you would."

I do too, one of the many reasons we get along so well. While Buzz doesn't live in the house, he's here every day in his unofficial role as housekeeper. He insisted on being given the title when I offered him a place to stay after Sue died. But he draws the line at being paid, so he lives in the cottage about a mile from the main house rent-free. He's my PA too when my virtual assistant is swamped and I often feel guilty for taking advantage of him, though he adamantly declares I'm not.

I know it kills him to live off Sue's life insurance policy, so I'll never tell him I subsidize those payments. I know what he'll say. He doesn't need it. But I need to pay. Guilt money for causing that accident, something I have to live with every single day.

Though we never talk about our pasts much, I know Cole's running from demons too. He used to be a lawyer in Chicago but quit a few months before his sister died. He hasn't told me why and I don't pry. I saw how angsty he got just mentioning his prior job as a legal eagle, so I let it be. I figure he'll tell me when he's ready. Considering we've been practically living together for five years, and he hasn't brought it up again, that's going to be never.

Buzz tugs on his flannel shirt and clears his throat. "Do you need anything in town?"

It looks like he can't wait to get out of here and I'm surprised. Buzz is a loner like me and rarely makes the trip into town unless absolutely necessary.

"You were just there, now you're heading back?"

His mouth kicks into a smirk. "You scared to be left alone with Mia?"

I scowl. Mia Samson doesn't scare me. The sway her reviews hold does. A situation I aim to rectify when I confront her shortly.

I ignore his question. "Unusual for you to make two trips in a day, especially when you'll be back in town tomorrow picking up the rest of the writers."

His eyebrows squeeze together in a frown. "Just some private business to attend to."

Buzz is a stand-up guy so when his gaze shifts away, I don't bother asking him anything else. We're best buddies but we respect each other's privacy so if he won't tell me what he's doing in town, that's okay. Besides, he'll tell me eventually. We won't get to have our usual Friday night beers watching football this week because of my house guests, which means Buzz will be keener to hang out next week. For a guy who barely speaks, give him a beer or two and I can't shut him up. I like it, because having a garrulous friend, even for one night a week, means I don't have to say much.

"Okay. See you later."

He hesitates, like he wants to say more, before giving a shake of his head. "Go easy on Mia, okay?"

"What's that supposed to mean?"

"I know you." He jabs a finger in my direction. "Having her arrive a day earlier than the others means you're up to something." Buzz's eyes narrow. "I looked her up, like I researched all the attendees, so I know she's a lauded book reviewer. What happened? Did she give you a bad review or something?"

'Or something' doesn't come close to what Mia Samson has done. "I'm not that petty."

Though maybe I am, because if I do half as bad a hatchet job on Mia's manuscript as she's done on a book close to my heart to teach her a lesson, that's exactly what I'll be.

Not that I'll deliberately tear down her work, but I'm going to be super critical, and I know from experience—when judging writing competitions in my early days—that not everyone handles feedback well. After receiving my first few abusive emails from disgruntled entrants, I bowed out of judging. Who needs the flack? I cop enough of that from readers every day.

"Whatever you're up to, think long and hard before you do anything you'll regret," Buzz says, disapproval lacing every word. "Non-disclosure agreements may be well and good, but if you make an enemy of this woman, don't forget she knows where you live."

I have no qualms about decimating Mia's manuscript. She can't disparage me any more than she already has. And as a wannabe writer, she'd be a fool to make me angry because the publishing world is small and she wouldn't risk getting a bad reputation.

"Stop worrying and go run your private errand." I point at the window. "And take care out there. Looks like the snow's coming down harder."

Buzz gives me a salute and a final warning glance I interpret as 'behave around Mia' before clomping through the kitchen to the back door.

I don't need his warnings. I'm a reasonable man. I won't ruin Mia's career. Which is more than I can say for her regarding mine.

Chapter Seven

MIA

My room is rustic. Wooden floors, wooden bed, wooden dresser, with a tiny brown melamine desk that looks like it's been squeezed in as an afterthought. Then again, I'm guessing the reclusive Axel Low doesn't entertain many house guests and he's thoughtfully added desks to the rooms for some private writing time.

A rectangular shaggy rug in duck-egg blue covers most of the floor and a duvet in a matching shade drapes the bed. The closet is minuscule and at odds with the surprising size of the room, almost as big as my entire studio back in Manhattan. I open a door next to the closet, grateful to find a small ensuite: shower, sink, toilet. One of my pet hates in college was sharing a bathroom and I assumed I'd have to do it here.

Then again, Axel Low is a multimillionaire several times over, so it shouldn't be a surprise he owns a massive house with at least seven bedrooms—his and one for each of his guests.

I can't quite fathom why a recluse would open his house like this, but rumor has it his publisher is pushing for higher sales volume on his next book and in today's age of rampant social media where one viral video can catapult an author's backlist title from a decade ago to the top of the charts, I'm assuming they want more publicity from Axel.

I don't bother unpacking. Cole said Axel would be in the living room and to introduce myself once I'd settled in. No time like the present. The house is blissfully warm, so I don't need a jacket. Lucky, because I accidentally left mine at home and only have the denim one I packed. I envisage lots of indoor time over the next week, but I'll need to buy one if I plan on exploring the town.

After a quick glance in the mirror to ensure I look presentable and not travel weary, I open my door and peek out into the hallway. I'm at the end and I pass another six doors on my way to the living room, situated at the front of the house. When I entered with Cole through the kitchen, the modern appliances, gleaming marble countertops and white cupboards had surprised me and now, walking through the house, it's even more incongruous against the rough-hewn ranch style of the rest of the place.

When I find the living room, I pause in the doorway, and I swear I swoon a little.

It's stunning.

Low sofas around a blazing fire, large floor cushions scattered nearby, reading lamps in various nooks, and cute little desks covered in new stationery. Bliss. As for the sweeping vista from the floor to ceiling windows—snow-covered trees dotting a virgin white landscape—could this place be any more inspirational?

I sigh and enter the room, crossing to the fire. The fireplace is surrounded by a bluestone mantel, with a mahogany bookshelf alongside it. I'm curious. What books does a best-selling author read for pleasure?

I lean forward to scan the creased spines but before I can scrutinize Axel's reading taste, I hear a thud behind me, followed by a muttered curse. I turn and forget to breathe.

The guy staring at me is hot.

More than hot. Exceptional.

Messy hair the color of dark chocolate spiking in all directions, like he eschews a brush or comb. Eyes that shift between blue and green; or as many romance authors I've read would say, cobalt and emerald. Sharp jaw covered in stubble. Cut-glass cheekbones. Faintest hint of a chin dimple. Nice.

Pity about the deep frown grooving his brow as he glares at me like I'm an unwelcome intruder.

"Hi, I'm Mia Samson, one of the winners of the writing competition." I sound way too perky, compounding my dorkiness when I raise my hand and wave.

His frown intensifies and his jaw clenches so hard I'm surprised I don't hear his teeth grinding.

I have no idea who this guy is but if he's one of Axel's minions who'll be around for the next week, I need to get him onside, so I flash my best smile. "Is Axel Low around? I'd like to introduce myself."

He shakes his head and takes a few steps forward and that's when I notice he's limping, and one of the desks is skewed. That must've been the thump I heard. No wonder he's grumpy. I would be too if I stubbed my toe.

"Ice should do the trick," I say, eliciting an arched eyebrow. I point to his right foot. "For a stubbed toe."

"I wouldn't have stubbed it if these stupid desks weren't in here," he mutters, gingerly flexing his foot.

Ah, maybe he's another of Axel's housekeepers. Or another PA. Or a chef. Stands to reason a busy man would have more than Cole on staff.

"Not a fan of writing?"

"Not a fan of writers," he says, giving me a quick perusal like I'm enemy number one.

"Hey, I have a real job too." I hold up my hands in surrender. "I'm not just a writer."

His eyes narrow, but not before I see a smolder of disapproval. "So writing isn't a real job?"

I feel like he's baiting me, and I'm tempted to reiterate I'm here to see/fangirl over Axel and don't have to tolerate his grouchiness. But it's not smart to alienate Axel's staff when I'm out to impress the great man, so I'll play nice.

"Not every writer is as lucky as your boss and can earn a good wage."

His expression morphs from disdain to confusion. "My boss?"

"Axel Low. Author extraordinaire. Word wunderkind. The page-turning prince."

I barely hear his muttered, "Save me," before he slides a cell from his back pocket.

"Are you calling Axel?"

"I'm calling my agent and telling her I can't do this."

I'm about to ask if he's a writer too when my common-sense kicks in. Nobody knows what Axel looks like and the speculation regarding his age implies he's over fifty because of his prose. That's why I envisaged him as a Stephen King type.

The guy scowling at me looks like he belongs in the pages of a romance novel rather than penning bestselling thrillers, and I try not to cringe at our less than stellar first meeting. I'd learned early in my career never to make assumptions, yet that's exactly what I've done here, assuming a guy this hot wasn't Axel. Could I be any dumber?

I quickly scan my brain for anything I might've said to offend and thankfully, come up empty. I have no idea why he hasn't introduced himself, but I plan to get what should've been an auspicious first meeting back on track.

"Mr. Low?" I cross the space between us and hold out my hand. "Sorry for the mix-up. I thought you were an employee—"

"Why? Because I don't walk around with a golden pen and a book with pages that turn themselves?"

I struggle not to gape. He's quoted one of my reviews for his release two years ago and his sarcasm confuses me. Is he poking fun at my flowery fan-girling or making a point that authors read reviews despite all protestations to the contrary?

Before I can ask, he slides his cell back into his pocket, his scowl replaced by a grimace. "I've been wanting to meet you, Ms. Samson."

He shakes my hand and releases it quickly, like he can't stand to touch me. I wish I could say the feeling is mutual but I'm struggling to refrain from grinning like an idiot after shaking the hand of such an illustrious author.

"Why?"

He doesn't answer immediately and his steely gaze bores into me, eliciting a slight chill despite the heat from the fire. I feel like he's sizing me up and finding me distinctly lacking.

"Because I have a lot to say about your work, as you've said about mine."

Not so cryptic after all and my heart leaps with hope. Is my partial that impressive? Did he devour my first three chapters and love them so much he'll give me a personal critique? It's what I hoped for but didn't dare get too excited. Just being in the same room as this guy, spending a week in his home writing, is a dream come true. Anything else is a bonus.

Thankfully, all my reviews for his books have been raves. Except the last one, which had been well below his usual standard, but I hadn't said anything particularly nasty. How awkward would this be if I'd said otherwise? But he's still giving off angry vibes, like he doesn't want me or any of the other writers anywhere near him, so I decide to try a little flattery.

"While I can't wait for you to critique my work, do you think you could sign a few books for me first? I packed half your backlist initially, but couldn't fit in enough clothes, so had to do a little rearranging and I've brought your first four releases with me. I'd love you to—"

"No."

Short. Sharp. Rude.

His neck is corded and he's tapping his foot, like he can't wait to escape my presence. So much for flattery. He's tall, at least a foot taller than me, and I hate having to crane my neck a little to stare at him, trying to get a read on my grumpy host.

When he doesn't say anything else and his frown deepens, I add, "Maybe later?"

After an interminable moment only broken by the crackling hiss of a log, he says, "I'll sign your copies on one condition."

"What is it?"

"You tell me where you get off using your poisonous vitriol to ruin an author's career."

Chapter Eight

AXEL

I've come on too strong.

I'd planned on being more circumspect in my approach; win Mia over, lull her into a false sense of security, then move in for the kill. But entering my living room to an impressive eyeful of denim-clad butt as she'd been bending forward to scope out my bookcase...I'd tripped over a desk and my mood had gone downhill from there.

I'm not a people person at the best of times. Grumpy. Recalcitrant. Moody. Labels I'm used to—courtesy of Buzz. Nobody else calls me out on my cantankerous demeanor because I don't socialize. The only people I speak to on a regular basis are Noni, Paula's aide, and my sister. Most of my dealings with Rolf, my editor, and Chrissie, my agent, are done via email. I rarely head into town so Buzz is it for human interaction. And it shows, considering my first awkward meeting with Mia.

To catch Mia off guard, I'd hoped to quash my inner grouch and lure her in with my scintillating charm.

Who am I kidding?

She's staring at me in open-mouthed shock after I've accused her of ruining authors' careers with her venomous reviews. Either she's never been called out before—which I find hard to believe—or it's my delivery that sucks. Probably the latter.

"Nothing to say?"

It's foolish to bait her, but I can't help it. I don't react well when I'm disarmed, and Mia Samson has done that; and how. She's prettier in person—hair the color of a Sugar Plain prairie in fall, all golds and russets, big green eyes, friendly smile— than online. While she has casual profile pics online for all to see, her social media accounts are private. Considering how she tears apart some authors' books, I'm not surprised. She'd be a prime target for nasty trolls.

"I've never said anything bad about your books." She's eyeing me with blatant confusion, like she can't figure me out. Join the club. It has many members, and I don't care.

"Doesn't mean you haven't ruined other writers' careers."

A tiny dent appears between her brows. "It's my job to review books and I'm as objective as I can be. It's a simple fact that not every book published is good. And I owe it to the New York Press readers to give my honest opinion."

It sounds like a spiel she's recited many times before. Which means I'm not the first author to confront her.

"I'm in publishing. I know how reviews work." I stalk to the fire and grab a poker. Her logic accentuates how unreasonable I'm being, and I need something to jab at, so I start prodding at the smoldering logs. "But your words hold more sway than most. Books you pump up go gangbusters, books you trash end up languishing. Surely you know that?"

For the first time since we met, I glimpse an angry spark in her eyes. She's obviously trying to impress me, to stay calm, probably with the aim to suck up. But I've hit a nerve and her eyes drift to the poker in my hand for a moment, like she's imagining skewering me with it.

"Readers are discerning. Some may value my reviews but for the most part, they can make their own decisions."

"Decisions heavily influenced by you."

She rolls her eyes and it's so cute I stifle a laugh. I don't want to be amused by her. I want to teach her a lesson.

"May I remind you, I'm here as a writer, a writer you chose as being worthy of this retreat because of the partial I submitted." She folds her arms, completely unaware it creates a tantalizing glimpse of cleavage that I struggle not to glance at. "So how about we focus on that, rather than my job as a reviewer?"

She pauses and the fire in her eyes flares into an inferno. "A job that pays the bills while I follow my real passion, writing." Her glance flicks around the room. "We can't all be as lucky as you to earn a living from something we love doing."

Okay, so she has a point. I'm so hellbent on chastising her that I forget she obviously enjoys writing—and is good at it, by what I've read. I'm annoyed that we have something in common, because I've been focused on disliking her and now, she's humanized.

"I've put in the hard work to get where I am."

"I'm sure you have. If anyone knows how tough it is to make it in this industry, it's another writer."

I'm intrigued against my better judgement. "Is that how you see yourself? As a writer?"

I've struck a nerve, as she squares her shoulders and those indigo flecks in her eyes glow with anger again. "Just because I'm not published yet doesn't make me less of a writer than... the next person."

Her pause implies she was going to say, 'less of a writer

than you' and I wonder why she changed it. But I'm not here to delve into the machinations of Mia's mind. I have an agenda and the rest of the day to get my point across before the others join us tomorrow.

"I didn't say you need to be published to be a writer."

"The implication was there." She lets out an exasperated huff almost as cute as her eye roll. "Look, I feel like we've got off on the wrong foot and you're misinterpreting everything I say. I'm thrilled to be here, and I can't wait to work with you, so how about we start again?"

She holds out her hand. "Hi, I'm Mia Samson. Fellow writer. And huge fangirl, though I'm trying to hide that part. Nice to meet you."

She has a point. I have more chance of getting her to change her mind about certain reviews if she's onside and I stop treating her like the enemy. But I'm not good at faking it so this will be tough. I must try, though. For Paula's sake.

"Axel Low. Writer. Recluse. Antisocial. Cynic." I take her hand to shake it and when our palms graze, there's a surprising zing of heat.

She feels it too, because her eyes widen imperceptibly, and she stares at our hands like she can't quite believe it.

That makes two of us. I have no room in my life for complications. And as Mia's big green eyes lock onto mine, I know she's one giant complication waiting to happen.

<h1 style="text-align:center">Chapter Nine</h1>

MIA

I'm mortified. Axel Low doesn't like me.

He's rude, condescending, and prickly, and I can't wait for the rest of the competition winners to arrive so I can blend in. So much for making the most of some one-on-one time with a bestselling author. The way he's staring at me, tomorrow can't come quick enough. Until then, I can sneak food from the kitchen and hide out in my room. Once I make a gracious escape now, that is.

"Want to know what I liked about your partial?" He shoves the poker back in its stand too hard and the contraption almost tips over, and by his scowl I assume spending time with me is the last thing he wants to do.

But his offer is too good to pass up. How many writers would give anything to have a one-on-one critique with this guy? Besides, I think it's his version of an olive branch and I'm glad I confronted the tension between us with that re-introduction, rather than continuing with the awkward accusation/defense thing we started with.

I have no idea where his animosity springs from because I'm right about one thing. I've never written a bad review about any of his books. I love them too much. He has a way of sucking the reader into a story that makes his books incredibly hard to put down. So, I'm assuming I've shredded one of his friend's tomes and that's what has him so angsty.

As for that spark when we shook hands, not going there. Nope. No matter how hot Axel is and how much he reminds me of Alex O'Loughlin, my favorite Aussie actor. I'm here to get a leg up in publishing and kickstart my writing career, not get a leg over him.

"I'd love to hear your feedback," I say in my best demure voice, but he eyes me suspiciously, like he's waiting for me to get snarky again.

"I have notes in my library."

"Library?"

He has a *library*? Oh my. Sexy best-selling author plus library equals I'm in so much trouble.

Libraries have been my go-to space since I was a child. They're the only place I felt truly safe. Hunkered down in a carrel or squeezed into a corner between bookshelves meant security for me. I know Mom tried her best after Dad died but when she started taking solace in a never-ending string of boyfriends who creeped me out, I'd get scared. Escaping in the pages of a book in the library a few doors from our apartment was the only way I could deal with my life.

"It's not that big," he says, and I hope I haven't been drooling over the thought of his library while lost in my memories.

"Lead the way."

He casts me one last confused look, like he can't work me out, before heading for the hallway. It's huge, with a skylight that casts everything in a whitish glow. It's still snowing outside and while I'd like to explore, I'll need a warmer coat and don't fancy asking my host for a loan of one of his or a lift into town to buy one.

We cross the hallway, and he opens a door. "Head in and make yourself comfortable. I'll get us something to eat. Cheese and crackers okay? Coffee?"

He's making an effort and I don't have the heart to tell him I'm probably the only writer on the planet who doesn't drink coffee. Love the aroma, hate the bitter aftertaste.

"Cheese and crackers sound perfect, but I'd prefer a water please."

"Cheap date."

When I bark out a laugh, he rears back like I've poked him in the eye, with a muttered, "Be back in a sec."

Shame the hot author doesn't have a sense of humor. Then again, if he did, I'd be a complete goner, because nothing turns me on as much as a killer wit. Swapping banter with a cute guy is my version of foreplay.

I step into the room and all the air in my lungs whooshes out in a rush.

Axel's library is breathtaking.

Pristine white bookshelves line three walls from floor to ceiling, packed with color-coded book spines, ranging from ebony to violet to crimson and every color in between. An expansive window, complete with reading nook covered in plump peacock blue velvet cushions, overlooks the snow-covered plain bordering the side of the property. And a huge glass-topped desk takes pride of place in the middle, like Axel enjoys being able to spin in his fancy ergonomic chair and survey all he has. There's a three-seater deep purple suede sofa complete with blanket behind his desk and I wonder if that's where he takes naps, waiting for his muse to arrive.

Unable to resist checking out the books, I start at the black spines first, expecting a mix of fantasy and paranormal. All the classics are there, along with a few additions that make me lean forward to investigate further. Names famous in erotica, along with several prominent indie authors who've made a name for themselves in the genre. Including Adele Lavash.

Publishers send prominent authors ARCs all the time to build hype for a release. But I can't imagine a best-selling crime author like Axel accepting a smutty advance reader copy from an indie like Adele. Bizarre.

Unless…is he a fan? Does he actually like her work? I know reading is subjective but…I suppress a shudder. Adele churns out smut because it pays well, and it shows. Her prose is lacking. Her plotting minimal. She's in it for the money. And while I have no qualms about doing what it takes to make money, it annoys me that so many more talented authors and their books go unrecognized when someone like Adele can publish anything and her avid readers will buy it regardless.

Not that I'm disparaging the genre either. I know I'll face the same ridiculous judgment from readers and reviewers who've never read romance but have strong opinions regardless if my regency ever gets published.

No, my problem with Adele Lavash, apart from the shortcomings in her books, is that I'm a teeny bit jealous.

What would it be like to have the time to publish several books a year, knowing you'd make enough money from each release to live like a queen? As opposed to working in a tiny cubicle opposite Jace, who wouldn't know brilliant literary fiction if it jumped onto his desk and danced.

I know my job dissatisfaction is growing in proportion to my word count. I want to spend more time writing so I'm starting to resent my day job. The one that pays my bills. The one I need to hold onto my studio apartment. The one I can't afford to leave unless I sell a book for a decent advance and become a frugal, impoverished full-time author.

"See anything you like?"

I jump and whirl around, heat flushing my cheeks. Silly, because I wasn't doing anything wrong, but a hint of gravel in Axel's tone implies he knows I was looking at the erotica. Not a big deal, but coupled with the memory of Jace insisting I should glom Adele Lavash's backlist to 'get me in the mood' I'm oddly embarrassed.

"You've got quite the eclectic collection." I gesture at the shelf behind me.

He shrugs. "I may not have time to read them all but I'm a book collector and being surrounded by them is comforting."

"I think so too."

Our gazes lock and I'm warmed by the understanding in his. Book lovers the world over recognize a kindred spirit when they see one and knowing Axel gets me—the part of me that's comforted around books—makes him more likeable.

He clears his throat and hands me a bottle of water. "Here. I'll get the platter."

"Thanks."

I unscrew the cap and take great gulps of water to ease the sudden tightness in my throat as I watch him leave the library; more precisely, I watch the way his ass moves in the tight denim molding it. Perfection.

He's back before I can analyze my wayward thoughts but thankfully, he doesn't glance my way, giving me time to get my blush under control.

When he places the platter on the desk and I get a glimpse of it, my stomach rumbles. "Wow. If that's your version of cheese and crackers, I'd hate to see a full charcuterie board."

"Too much?" His mouth kicks into a rueful grin and I'm struck anew by how gorgeous he is when he's not glowering at me.

"Not at all." I cross the room to take a dried apricot and pop it into my mouth. He's gone all out, with salami, prosciutto, olives, sun-dried tomatoes, pesto, and hummus accompanying the brie, camembert, cheddar, and gouda. "I'll need sustenance while you give me feedback."

One of his eyebrow's arches. "Aren't you the least bit concerned that what I have to say might ruin your appetite?"

"Nope. Too hungry for that." I pop a garlic-infused olive into my mouth and sigh, and Axel laughs, a full-bodied chuckle that makes the lines around his eyes fan out in an intriguing map and my thighs clench.

I am in definite trouble.

"I'll grab my coffee, then we can start."

I manage a garbled "okay," and focus on stuffing as much cheese and cured meat into my mouth as I can before he returns. The queasiness in my stomach must be from hunger and nothing to do with how darn appealing Axel is with every passing moment.

I don't like moody men as a rule. Too much baggage. So it had been easy not to like Axel after our fraught first meeting in the living room. But here, now, surrounded by books and warmth from the central heating and an author who laughs like he means it...I'm in danger of falling for more than Axel's way with words.

Then again, I'm sure he has plenty of other readers crushing on him. What's one more?

"Right, let's get down to business," he says, closing the door and engulfing us in unexpected intimacy. Or maybe that's just my interpretation, because when a sexy writer says, *'let's get down to business'* I'm thinking of more than a critique. Much more.

With my cheeks burning for the third time in as many minutes, he pins me with a curious glance. "Everything okay?"

"Yes. Fine. Thanks."

My voice sounds strangled, so I stuff a wedge of brie into my mouth.

With a last curious glance my way, he picks up a folder from his desk and sits on the sofa. He's holding his coffee in his other hand and takes a sip, waiting for me to sit too. Next to him. On the soft sofa that looks way too comfy. In this perfect room. With my wildly inappropriate thoughts of erotica and Axel.

Clamping down on my vivid imagination, I perch on the edge of the sofa and clutch my bottled water so hard the plastic crumples a little.

"Mediocre," he says, flipping open the folder, and just like that the imaginary sensual bubble around us bursts.

Is a full-blown critique from one of the best thriller writers in the world on the first three chapters of my domestic suspense novel really what I want if his first impression of my writing is mediocre?

Chapter Ten

AXEL

Trite. Clichéd. Unoriginal. Sentences too long. Verbose. Unrealistic. Reads like a soap opera. Too much tell, not enough show.

All criticisms I wanted to lay on Mia. None of them true, but to give her a taste of her own medicine, to give her a feel of what it's like to be on the receiving end of a harsh critique.

Not that she'd understand the real devastation of a release tanking courtesy of her cutting criticism, but I want to prove a point before I tell her about Adele.

However, my plan hits a snag when I get the first word out. She visibly flinches when I say 'mediocre' and in that instant, I know I can't do it.

It's not in my nature to tear down someone's work, because I know how hard it is to get words written on paper let alone complete several chapters. As for the synopsis that accompanied her submission, it's far better than anything I can come up with. I loathe synopsis writing with a passion. I do it because Chrissie demands it before she pitches my next idea to my publisher, though I'm luckier than most in that my publisher knows whatever I come up with will sell a lot of books and, in turn, make us all a lot of money.

Not that Mia's synopsis and partial doesn't need work. It does, but the natural snark in her voice makes for compelling reading and I can't lie to her. It wouldn't sit well with me. Besides, the writing gods might believe in writer's block even if I don't and I can't tempt fate.

So I shelve my plan to teach her a lesson by disparaging her work. I'll come up with another way to get my point across.

"What I mean is, the motivation of your protagonist's sister is mediocre and needs a lot of work," I say, and her shoulders relax, the tension pinching her mouth easing. "If you want to throw suspicion on several villains and get the reader to wonder who's behind the threats, you need to solidify the sister, because at the moment it seems obvious that she's the baddie."

"That sounds doable." She points to a stack of sticky notes on my desk. "Mind if I take notes?"

"Go ahead. I haven't marked up the manuscript because I don't have the time to do it for all six of you, but I intend on giving detailed verbal feedback."

Her wide-eyed stare is filled with admiration, and I struggle not to squirm in the face of her open adoration. I don't want her to look at me like I'm about to bestow a great gift. I'm blunt at the best of times, but after seeing her visibly flinch when I said 'mediocre' a few moments ago, I know I'll have to temper my critique.

I'm ashamed to think I invited her here a day early to teach her a lesson by disparaging her work. Who does that? I'm a grown-ass man, not a petulant kid. I'm under a lot of pressure, with contract negotiations looming for my next book and a hike in Paula's fees at Sunny Pines, but that's no excuse. Thank goodness I came to my senses before it's too late. Buzz is right. Getting Mia Samson offside can have far-reaching consequences and I'd be better off befriending her rather than antagonizing.

"Detailed verbal feedback sounds great." She picks a green pen from the countless colors I have in a holder on my desk and grabs a yellow sticky note pad. "What else?"

I struggle not to stare as her eyes glow with enthusiasm, lighting up her entire face and taking it from pretty to stunning. "There's a fair bit of telling not showing in the first chapter, but that can be resolved by leaping straight into the inciting incident."

"You think I should start the story when Brooke receives the first threatening email?"

"Exactly. Cut the intro where you tell us how she's feeling a vague sense of menace."

She scribbles furiously for a few moments, giving me a chance to study her. I notice there are more red streaks amid the gold in her hair than I first thought, and she gnaws on her bottom lip when deep in thought. She also has a callous on the third finger of her right hand, where the pen rests, and I wonder if she kept a journal as a teen. Paula did and she has a similar callous.

Thinking about my sister and how she can barely string two words together these days let alone write a coherent sentence makes my throat tighten.

I need to make more money to afford Paula's medical bills and the more money Adele Lavash makes, the more money I do.

But my association with Adele is a well-guarded secret and I don't want to tip Mia off too early. I need to gain her trust, get her to see me as the upstanding author I am, so she takes my request more seriously.

"What else?" Mia taps her pen against the sticky notes, staring at me expectantly.

I recognize the slight glaze in her eyes; I sport something similar when I'm in the zone, when the ideas can't come quick enough, and I jot down random plot points and twists and scenes that need to happen.

It's disarming, seeing how enthused she is and that we share a common bond: a love of creating. I don't want to like Mia too much. She's already caught me off guard with how attractive she is and the last thing I need is to find more things to like about her.

"Right, here's what I think."

My gruff tone doesn't deter her and she continues to stare at me, pen poised, so I proceed to outline exactly what I think does and doesn't work in the first three chapters of her manuscript. Her pen doesn't stop, flying across the sticky notes, until she has a decent stack in front of her.

I should hate doing this. I hadn't been looking forward to critiquing the winners' manuscripts at all. But turns out, I get so absorbed in giving feedback and debating changes with Mia, I lose track of time and the only way I know a few hours have passed is by the twinge in my lower back. It's the same twang I get when I'm in the zone and having a rare day of countless pages, when eight thousand words pour out of me and I can't stop.

I stand and stretch, unable to stifle a groan. Man, I'll be forty in two years and I'm starting to feel it. In comparison, Mia leaps off the sofa and bends her back in an elegant arch that reminds me of Mr. Darcy, Buzz's cat, who spends more time in my house than Buzz's cottage.

"That was amazing, and I can't thank you enough..." she trails off, surprise raising her brows when she glances over my shoulder. "Uh, how long have we been doing this?"

"Why?"

"Because fall has turned to winter."

I turn to see what she's pointing at, and I'm shocked to see the snowstorm obliterating the view that's as familiar to me as my favorite keyboard with the E, T and S keys worn away.

"The forecasters mentioned the possibility of an unseasonal blizzard but..." I shake my head. "I've never seen anything like this in the years I've lived here."

She cocks her head. "I can't hear a thing. Looks like the wind's howling out there."

"Double-glazing and concrete walls covered by bricks. Great insulators."

"It's like being shut off from the world," she says, a small smile playing about her mouth, and as my gaze lingers there, I have an insane urge to kiss her.

Rattled, I take a few steps away from her and pat my back pocket; to find my cell missing, belatedly realizing I left it in the kitchen. "I need to check in with Buzz and see how bad the blizzard is in town."

"Okay. I might go to my room and start inputting some of these changes into my manuscript."

My nod is brusque. The sooner I get rid of her the better, because once the impulse to kiss her lodged in my brain, I can't shake it. It's off-putting because I haven't dated since Paula's accident let alone thought about a woman. My days are spent hunched over my keyboard, writing as many words as humanly possible, my nights too. Buzz has dragged me into town for a beer at the bar a few times, but I hate being surrounded by people who expect me to be sociable.

I have no time for small talk. I have a low tolerance for BS, and it shows. Even if a woman was interested in me, she'd take one look at my permanent glower and run for the hills.

It makes me wonder, what is it about Mia that had me letting down my guard for the last few hours to the extent I lost track of time?

Writing is my passion, so it figures I like talking about it, but what I enjoyed most about critiquing her work is the back and forth we did, the debating of ideas, the challenge of finding flaws and solving problems. It's unnerving, to realize I might not be such a hermit after all.

She hasn't moved a step and is staring at me, and I figure she's waiting for a response.

"Sure. Buzz should be back soon, so we'll have dinner in an hour if that suits?"

She glances at her watch. "You eat at five-thirty?"

"Too early?"

"Not if you're a fan of early bird specials."

"Well, I'm probably a decade or more older than you."

"I'm twenty-eight."

"Yep. I've got ten years on you."

An impish gleam lights her eyes. "Positively ancient."

She's joking but, in that moment, I feel that decade between us stretching interminably. What would it be like to be twenty-eight again, without a care beyond bugging Chrissie every five minutes to ask if the publishing houses who entered a furious bidding war for my first book had made their final offer?

Life had been simpler then. I'd been in demand as a carpenter, building boutique homes for people who couldn't afford the big-name architects, while writing on the side, something I'd done since my late teens when pouring my thoughts onto paper was the only way I coped with my grief after my folks died. Never in my wildest dreams had I thought I'd land an agent, let alone a six-figure advance for my first book after a rigorous auction. I'd been flying high then, fueled by my self-importance.

But it had all come crashing down the night I signed my first contract and Paula had suffered the fallout. It became imperative to keep my identity secret to protect her. Ironic, that I'm still doing it, but for a different reason.

"You know I'm kidding, right?" Mia touches my arm and I jump as if short-circuited. "About you being ancient?"

Once again, I've drifted off, lost in my thoughts, and I grit my teeth against the urge to blurt an unnecessary apology. "I eat early because I like to get another four hours writing done after dinner. While you and the others are here, I'll expect you to fit in with my schedule."

"Of course." The gleam in her eyes fades and I inwardly curse for being so curt. "Do you really write all day, then do another four hours after dinner?"

"Yes. That's what real writers do."

The implication is clear—she's doing this as a hobby—and my barb hits home if the stiffening of her shoulders and the compressing of her lips is any indication. I feel like a jerk for demeaning her like that, but I need to do something to re-establish distance between us; before I do something crazy and ask her to come back here after dinner and we can do some more brainstorming together.

"I'll see you later," she mutters, and I watch her go with a bewildering mix of regret and yearning.

Chapter Eleven

MIA

I stomp to my room, torn between wanting to march back to the library and give Mr. High and Mighty a verbal spray he'll never forget, and kicking something. I settle for slamming my bedroom door.

I turn, to find a black cat sitting on my bed, wearing the same supercilious expression Axel had when he dismissed me a few moments ago.

I hate cats. Though hate may be too strong. It's just that Mom loved them and lavished a hell of a lot more affection on the two tabbies we had than she ever did on me. And those two smug creatures knew it. Incongruously named Spot and Rover—Mom had a warped sense of humor too—they would wind their way through my legs whenever I got home from school and I would grit my teeth against the feel of their fur tickling my skin, because I knew they were faking it. The minute Mom turned her back they'd be swiping at me with their claws unsheathed, like they knew I was competing with them for attention.

I swear Mom fed them better too. While I'd be lucky to scrounge up a frozen meal, those darn cats ate the best tinned tuna. And Mom cried buckets when they both died within a month of each other, while she waved me off to college without a hint of a tear.

"Shoo." I wave my hands in a pinwheeling motion and the cat's smirk intensifies.

It doesn't move a muscle and I approach warily, not liking the gleam in its amber eyes one bit. Feral doesn't come close to describing how this cat is staring at me, like it's about to take a flying leap and land on my face.

"Go on, scram." I clap my hands and it stands, arches its back in a stretch, and daintily leaps off the bed, stalking toward the door without a backward glance.

I open the door to let the cat out, to find Axel standing on the other side with his hand raised as if he's about to knock.

The cat lets out a plaintive meow and rubs itself against Axel's leg, and for an insane moment I'm jealous of the feline. Then I remember how moody Axel is, how he morphs from sexy enthusiastic writer to rude grumpy guy in a second, and I harden my heart against the teensiest shimmer of a crush I developed while he'd spent the last few hours giving me an invaluable critique.

"I see you've met Mr. Darcy," he says, eyeing the cat with the same mistrust I had a few moments ago.

I nod. "Aren't you taking the writer cliché to extremes, with the cat and the name?"

"He's not my cat." He gives a mock shudder. "I can't stand cats, but he belongs to Buzz, and Buzz spends more time here than in his cottage during the day, so Mr. Darcy makes himself at home. As for the name, Buzz rescued the cat not long after he moved into the cottage and said the name is a reminder of his past. He didn't elaborate and I didn't push."

I don't like that we have something else in common—our mutual loathing of cats. It makes me identify with him and I don't want to do that. I need to remember why I'm here—to learn from the best—and not want to delve into what makes this enigmatic man tick.

"By your expression, I take it you're not a fan either?"

I grimace. "Is it that obvious?"

"Do you like dogs?"

"Love them."

"That's okay then." The glimmer of a smile hovers and I wonder how breathtakingly gorgeous he would be if he relaxed long enough for a full-blown grin. "Otherwise, I'd think you have no soul."

The faintest hum is back, the tension between us stretching taut in our awkward pause, and I rush to fill the silence. "Was there something you wanted?"

He shifts his weight onto the balls of his feet and thrusts his hands into his pockets, discomfort etched across his face. "I wanted to apologize."

"For?"

"The way I ended our session before." He winces. "I didn't mean to imply you're not a real writer."

"Yet you did." I cross my arms and lean against the door, my inner imp wanting to make him squirm. "I think you're an amazing writer and it's a dream come true for me to get feedback from you, but if you have a problem with me, perhaps it's best we get it out in the open now?"

I can't read the shifting emotions in his eyes. There's something he's not telling me and considering I write suspense I love solving a good mystery.

"I'm not a people person," he eventually says, but I know there's more to it.

I'm curious, but now's not the time to push for answers. I can't afford to antagonize him, not when the few hours feedback I just got will take my manuscript to the next level, and I want him to read the rest of what I've written.

I also want to pick his brains about any contacts he may have in the romance genre. Not that I'm going to reveal my passion for regency romance just yet, but the more information I can glean from him, the easier it's going to be for me to get published. I hope. And that means playing nice with the grouchy author.

"Well, considering you're going to be hosting me and another five people shortly, may I suggest you loosen up a little?"

His face screws up, whether at the thought of more people invading his home or at my sass, I have no idea.

"Uh, there's something I have to tell you."

Once again, I can't get a read on him, but he's not happy. His back is ramrod straight and he can't look me in the eye.

"What is it?"

"I got a text from Buzz about an hour ago that I didn't see until I checked my cell." His brows pull together. "We're cut off."

"Cut off from what?"

"Everything." He points to my window where the curtains are drawn. "We're snowed in."

I shrug. I'm stuck in a sprawling luxurious ranch-style house with a best-selling author. There are worse things. "That's okay, unless you tell me you're out of food."

"We have enough food to feed an army." He shakes his head. "That's not the problem."

"Then what is?"

"The blizzard is forecasted to intensify, which means we might be snowed in." He pauses for emphasis. "For a week."

That's the moment I realize I'm trapped, alone, with a

man who doesn't want me here, a man I find infinitely appealing.

Chapter Twelve

AXEL

Usually, being snowed in wouldn't bother me. A week or more of uninterrupted writing time, with unreliable wi-fi access meaning I don't have to converse with Chrissie or Rolf, my editor, is practically a dream come true.

But that dream has turned into a nightmare with Mia Samson stuck in my house too.

The funny thing is, when I told her the bad news, she'd been stoic, but I hadn't missed the glint of excitement in her eyes.

And that doesn't bode well for me.

Because the kicker is, I know where that excitement stems from.

Good old-fashioned lust.

I know because I feel it too, that tenuous connection, an underlying simmer of...*something* between us that could detonate if we let it.

And I can't go there, no matter how much I'm tempted.

I have more important things to worry about than my dormant libido, and with Mia thankfully holed up in her room, I can call Paula. I'm anxious, because I check in at least twice a week and with this snowstorm, the wi-fi can drop out at any minute. I have a generator but during storms the wi-fi is sketchy at best so I can't imagine it's going to hold out long in a blizzard.

The staff at Sunny Pines are expecting my call so when I close the library door, sit at my desk, flip open my laptop and hit the call button, it doesn't take long for Paula's face to pop up on the screen. My heart gives a familiar squeeze when I see the vacant look in my sister's eyes; eyes once filled with so much vibrance.

"Hey, Sis." I wave. "Great to see you."

The corners of Paula's mouth pull up into a semi-smile and it lightens my heart like it usually does. The fact she can recognize me and comprehend what I'm saying is a vast improvement on the early days after the accident, when her brain had suffered so much trauma that the docs weren't even sure she'd make it. At times I still wish I could have her here with me, but the extent of her physical and cognitive impairment means that's impossible, so it's some consolation I can pay for the premier special accommodation facility for patients like Paula, somewhat relieved she's being cared for by experts who are doing a far better job than I ever could.

But it does little for the nagging guilt I can't shift no matter how hard I try.

Paula's in this condition because of me.

Noni, Paula's primary caregiver, pops onto the screen beside her. "Hey, Axel. How are you?"

"Good."

A blatant lie but I keep up the pretense for Paula's sake. I haven't been good in a long time.

"How's the building business treating you?"

"Busy." The lie slides easily from my lips.

To Noni and the rest of the world, I'm Axel Moore, carpenter. When I came up with the pseudonym Axel Low, I stuck with my first name so I wouldn't get tripped up, but I know that—combined with my voice on the literary podcast and the gem I'd inadvertently let slip—was what alerted Paula's ex to our whereabouts.

"We've been busy too, haven't we, Paula?" Noni smiles and I've never been more grateful to the fifty-something nurse when Paula leans into her, a peaceful expression on her face. Knowing my sister has someone she trusts completely and is happy being looked after by is a weight off my shoulders. "Want to show Axel what you made?"

Paula holds up a poster board punctured with tiny holes, where brightly colored dots have been pressed into it in the shape of a rudimentary black cat.

"Mr. Darcy?" I ask and Paula nods, pride that I've recognized her efforts making her skin flush. And in that moment, I'm glad that annoying cat leaped onto my desk the last time we video-called if it's prompted Paula to do this.

"We've been reading books about cats too," Noni says, and a familiar pain lances me. Paula used to be my beta reader, devouring everything I wrote and giving me copious notes. These days, she can barely recognize letters let alone read a full sentence.

"That's great." I force a smile, when inside I'm fighting a familiar ache that's spreading across my chest. An ache of loss, regret, and what might've been if I'd done things differently and hadn't agreed to that interview that led to my sister's life being turned upside down. "Just to let you know, we're having a freak snowstorm here at the moment, so depending on the wi-fi situation, I might not be able to call again later this week."

"No problems. We're all good here." Noni gently squeezes Paula's shoulders. "You take care in that storm, okay?"

"Shall do."

Paula's lost interest in my call and is fiddling with the dots that make up the cat, her bangs falling across her eyes like it used to when she'd been a kid. I did everything in my power to protect her growing up and it still wasn't enough, and that's something I'll have to live with every damn day.

"Bye, Paula. Love you." I kiss my fingertips and press them against the screen in the same way I end all our calls.

Sometimes she tries to copy me, but the effort required for eye to hand to mouth coordination is too hard. Today, she's disinterested, and I end the call before Noni and my sister see the tears filling my eyes.

Chapter Thirteen

MIA

When I'm this jittery only one person can talk me down.

Rosie.

Besides, while Axel reassured me he has a generator so we shouldn't lose power, he mentioned the wi-fi is spotty during storms and we may lose contact with the outside world at any time. It wouldn't bother me usually. Heck, how many writers worldwide would give anything to be snowed in with Axel Low?

Personally, it's a dream come true. If it wasn't for the teensy-weeny issue of my burgeoning crush.

I can't afford to screw up this opportunity but that's exactly what will happen if I give in to the relentless impulse to see if I can get him to lighten up in the best possible way.

He's hot. Better than the sexiest book boyfriend. I blame those elusive fictional men on my failure to find a guy who's good enough. Turns out, real men aren't alpha with a beta core. If they're alpha, they're usually arrogant and self-absorbed. And the beta guys don't provide me with enough of a challenge, so I'm destined for dating disasters and that's where Rosie comes in.

She'll get me out of this funk. She has in the past. She'll talk sense and I'll listen.

At least, that's what I hope.

She's having issues with the video call feature on her ancient cell, so I pull up my favorites list and tap the first name, hers. Speaks volumes for my social life that I have three people listed: Rosie, Jace, and Mom. And I rarely hit the last name.

Rosie answers on the second ring, like she's been clutching her cell waiting for my call. "Tell me everything, babe."

"Hello to you too."

She makes a pfft sound. "I'm dying to know about the mysterious Axel Low. And if he's the troll you expected him to be, how about the other writers there? Any hotties?"

Predictably, Rosie hasn't let me get a word in. I love my verbose friend because she's a nice foil for me. I stick to the less is more mantra when chatting. I'm a listener, always have been. Maybe that's why someone like Axel fascinates me so much? I want to plumb his hidden depths.

"Do you think about anything but guys?"

This time, she blows a raspberry. "You forget, I'm a year older than you and turning thirty soon."

"So? You'll be flirty thirty." I lower my voice and snigger. "Or dirty thirty."

"Whatever. If I'm still single by then, I'm moving to Australia."

"Why Australia?"

"Hello? Have you seen Chris Hemsworth?"

I swear my muscles relax just listening to my friend. Even her prattle is calming. "Speaking of hot Aussies...turns out, Axel looks like Alex O'Loughlin."

There's a long silence before Rosie's squeal has me easing my cell away from my ear.

"No way."

Remembering how the flecks in Axel's eyes glow when he's passionate about something—like talking about writing—makes my cheeks flush. "Yeah. Turns out he's only thirty-eight, so not quite the vintage I imagined from his prose."

"Axel and Alex. Isn't that funny?"

I can think of many words to describe either of those men. Funny isn't one of them.

"What's he like, apart from drop-dead gorgeous?" Rosie asks.

I want to say 'nice' but that's not exactly true. And way too inadequate to describe a guy of Axel's caliber.

"He's...intense."

"Oooh, what does that mean?"

Rude. Standoffish. Moody. But oddly, I don't want to disparage him to my best friend, especially when I barely know him.

Yet I know enough, like the way he absentmindedly twirls a pen between his thumb and forefinger while critiquing, how his tongue flicks out to sweep his top lip after the first sip of coffee, and the faintest dimple that appears when he smiles.

It's crazy, because we're virtually strangers, but spending the last few hours cocooned in his library, listening to him, spellbound by his every word as he went through my partial like he really understands my plot, has made me go a little loopy for the guy.

"Babe? If you don't tell me what intense means, I'm going to come down there and see for myself. And I'm pretty sure you don't want me cramping your style."

Rosie doesn't cramp my style. She obliterates it. Not that I have style, per se, but any time we go out to a bar and meet cute guys, she never fails to embarrass me by regaling them with tales of my dorkiness: working on the college newspaper, my total ineptitude on rollerblades, how I barely swing my arms when I jog. If she wasn't so adorable, I'd hate her.

"You can't come here."

She snorts. "Is that a challenge? Because you know what I love more than tall, tattooed guys, right? A challenge."

I hadn't planned on telling Rosie I'm snowed in because I know she'll make too much of it, especially now I've revealed how hot Axel is. So much for her talking me down from my wee crush. Once she hears this, she'll go mad.

"You can't come here because we're snowed in."

"Bummer. Must be weird being stuck with a bunch of strangers, even if Axel Low is hot."

I brace for a signature Rosie squeal and move the cell away from my ear again. "That's the thing. I'm the first to arrive."

There's a pause as she digests the implication behind what I've just said. "It's just you and him?"

Hesitating isn't going to prevent the level of excitement my admission is about to elicit. "Yeah."

Her squeal is so loud I swear my cell vibrates. "You are so going to bone the hot author."

Heat flushes my cheeks at the thought. "Don't be ridiculous. I can't blur professional lines."

Rosie chuckles. "What professional lines? You're not working together. You won a competition to spend some time picking his brains. That's not work. That's luck." She makes smooching sounds. "And now you're about to get even luckier."

An image of his living room springs to mind—blazing fire, low-lit lamps, large cushions on the floor, the two of us stuck here—and I squeeze my thighs together. "You're not helping, Rosie Posey."

"I'm the last person to talk you out of anything, you should know that by now." She pauses and I can almost hear the wheels turning in her head. "Wait a minute. Is that why you called? You've got the hots for Mr. Intense, and you wanted me to talk you out of it?"

She knows me too well. "Something like that."

Her laughter is loud and boisterous, my friend to a tee. "I've got two words for you. Do him."

She has no idea how much I want to, so I reach for a subject guaranteed to distract. "Jace is having a party next week. You should come."

"I know..." She realizes her mistake a second too late and groans. "I know you warned me off him, but I can't help myself. You know I love a bad boy."

"You love all boys," I say, knowing Rosie is smart enough to see through Jace's BS but hoping she doesn't get hurt regardless.

"Did he say something to you about us talking this morning?"

"No, but I know you. I warned you off him, so I knew you'd contact him."

"Smart-ass," she mutters. "Relax, babe. I know he's only good for a little fun. It's not like I want to marry the guy."

Now it's my turn to groan. "Please. Anyone but him."

"No other hotties in the wilds of Sugar Plain that I can corrupt?"

Cole is tall, dark, and handsome in a lumberjack kind of way, but the chances of Rosie setting foot in Nebraska are nil, so he's safe.

"Does that mean you're willing to leave Manhattan if I find you a local stud?"

"No freaking way."

We laugh in unison. Rosie's a city girl through and through. The furthest she ventures from Manhattan is the Hamptons and that's only under great sufferance. The newspaper CEO has a house there and he rents it out to staff for one weekend each over summer. A great perk I take advantage of.

"Anyway, I must go. Axel gave me some excellent ideas for my manuscript that I want to implement."

Rosie huffs out a sigh. "Don't work too hard. Especially when you're stuck with the hot Aussie lookalike. What's his house like?"

"As big and impressive as the rest of him," I deadpan, and she laughs.

"That's my girl. Keep me posted, okay?"

I don't tell her I may not get the opportunity if the cellular coverage cuts out. "Sure. And you take it easy on Jace. I have to work with him, remember?"

"I promise to be gentle." She snickers. "Take care, babe."

"You too."

Rosie hangs up and I'm left staring at my cell, wondering if it's such a bad thing to be cut off from the outside world completely.

Especially if it means I have Axel Low all to myself.

Chapter Fourteen

AXEL

Writing is my full-time job and I treat it as such. I don't wait for the fabled muse to strike. I sit at my desk every single day, do a quick re-read of the last chapter I wrote, then pick up where I left off. I'm a plotter so I know where the story is heading and using digital color-coded index cards for different characters means I can see at a glance which scene comes next.

Except today.

My entire routine is off, courtesy of a disruptive book reviewer who is currently residing in one of the bedrooms, while I'm sitting at my desk and staring out the window rather than focusing on giving my villain a more convoluted backstory.

I rarely do this. Dither. Ponder. I don't listen to music while I write, I don't snack, and I sure as hell don't daydream.

This is all Mia's fault.

Talking about her manuscript, delving into her plot, seeing her visible excitement—glowing eyes, small smile playing about her mouth, flying fingers as she scrawled notes nonstop—has thrown me off my game and she's all I can think about.

On the rare occasion my plot isn't working, I take a break and go find Buzz to provide a suitable distraction. We chop wood or play a video game or stream a thriller. But Buzz isn't around, and I'm stuck with my tempting enemy.

I can't lose sight of that. No matter how delectable Mia is, or how sweet, she *is* my enemy.

I need to discuss Adele Lavash with her. Get her to see reason. The non-disclosure agreement she signed prohibits her from revealing anything that is discussed during her time here, and considering she's the only one I'm telling, she'd be a fool to blab to anybody and risk a lawsuit. It would end her career before it's begun, and I doubt she'll do that.

But I don't trust easily and I'm worried that once I reveal my secret, she'll use it against me somehow.

I shake my head and return to staring at the blank page in front of me. This is usually the easy part of writing for me, the first few chapters, when I can't get the words out fast enough. It's exhilarating, having scenes I see in my mind transform into words on a page. A few sentences at first, that soon run into paragraphs, and from there I'm flying, lost in a make-believe world that's far better than the one I live in.

But I'm not flying today. I'm grounded, and no matter how hard I will the words onto the page...nothing.

With a frustrated growl I push away from my desk, stand, and stretch overhead. Not that my muscles have had a chance to stiffen up, considering I've barely been sitting for thirty minutes.

I could try reading. Getting lost in a story relaxes me, but as I scan my towering to-be-read pile—more like shelf upon shelf of unread books—nothing grabs my attention.

Maybe a snack will help free up my creativity—yeah, right

—but as I open the door, Mr. Darcy is sitting there, staring at me with knowing eyes.

"What do you want?"

In response, the cat stalks into the library and leaps nimbly onto my desk—where I repeatedly dislodge him from—and curls up, still eyeing me balefully.

"I thought cats were supposed to be smart," I mutter, crossing the room to pick him up and deposit him on the sofa instead.

I get a hiss for my trouble. "Yeah, you and me both, buddy. It's that kind of day."

Mr. Darcy gives a desultory flick of his tail and I realize I'll be stuck with this cat until Buzz gets back, whenever that is. The blizzard hasn't let up—if anything it has intensified—and I'm glad Buzz stocks cat food here as well as the cottage, considering how much time Mr. Darcy spends here. I may not like the cat, but I don't want it to starve.

"You hungry?"

Mr. Darcy licks a paw and swipes at his ear, completely disinterested in anything I have to say.

"Okay, suit yourself. But I'm going to fix dinner for Mia and me so if you want something, you know where to find us."

The thought of sitting across the table from Mia and sharing an intimate dinner for two makes me break into a sweat. As if the last few months haven't been tough enough, it looks like the weather gods have turned against me too and I'm stuck with her for however long it takes for the snow to ease and the plows to get through.

As I glance at Mr. Darcy, I swear that smug cat is grinning.

Chapter Fifteen

MIA

After my call with Rosie, I manage to input a few of Axel's suggestions into the first chapter of my manuscript. The working title is Kill for You and features two sisters, twins, who will do anything for their sibling. It's more domestic noir than suspense but maybe that's because my characters are so twisted, they do bad things even when I don't want them to.

Axel's suggestion about layering the backstory for one of the sister's is spot on. She needs to be more likeable, more relatable, so readers don't assume she's the villain immediately. I know I need more red herrings too, but this is my first attempt at writing a thriller and I'm flying by the seat of my pants—I'm a pantser, a funny term coined by writers for those who don't plot their stories.

The thing is, I tried plotting, but I got bored. I like not knowing where my characters will take me and how the plot will unravel. It's half the fun. Ironic, because in real life, I like order. I have the ARCs that need reading and reviewing carefully dated, I never miss a deadline, I have alerts set on my cell for everything from paying bills to my annual teeth clean, and I schedule socializing around my professional life. I like the routine. It's my safety net. Because without order there's anarchy.

Just ask my mom.

There's a knock on my door and I glance at the time in the top right-hand corner of my laptop. It's after six, which means that'll be Axel checking in to see if I want dinner. I do and I don't. I'm hungry but I can't face eating while sitting across from him, envisaging him as dessert.

This is crazy. I'm not this person. The kind of girl who yearns. My life is orderly, remember? That's why I like the conciseness of dating apps. No muss no fuss. But deep down, in a place I barely acknowledge, that place that wants more out of life, I know thinking about Axel in anything other than professional terms is one big mess waiting to happen.

With a sigh, I close my laptop, and do a quick check in the mirror hanging over the dresser before opening the door. "Hey."

It's lucky I don't have a lot to say and managed that one syllable, because my throat tightens as I take in the sheer magnetism of Axel. It's not what he's wearing—though I am partial to faded denim and soft cotton on a guy—but the vibe he emanates: a distinct hands-off, which makes me want to do the opposite.

"Get a lot of work done?"

I nod. "Most of the first chapter, which is good. It's much tighter now, thanks to you."

"No worries."

By the deep groove between his brows, that's a lie. Axel appears perpetually worried, and I wonder what a successful guy like him at the top of the publishing game has to be concerned about.

"Are you hungry?" He jerks a thumb over his shoulder. "We can eat in the kitchen if you like, keep things informal?"

"Sounds good to me."

"I've heated some cannelloni and garlic bread, and we can throw together a salad if you like?"

A vision of the two of us shredding lettuce, chopping cucumbers, and dicing tomatoes springs to mind and I know I can't do it. The less 'couple' things we do together, the better.

"The carbs are enough." I pull my door shut so Mr. Darcy doesn't go getting any ideas again and fall into step beside him. "How about you? How many words did you get written?"

He doesn't answer and I hold up my hand. "Don't tell me. I bet your usual word count is about five thousand per session. Am I right?"

"Pretty much," he says, his tone gruff. "But I didn't get much done this afternoon."

I inhale sharply and slap my hand against my mouth in fake outrage. "Don't tell me the great Axel Low gets writer's block like the rest of us?"

The corners of his mouth twitch, like he's trying to suppress a laugh. "I don't believe in it. I prefer to think if I plant my butt in a chair and put my fingers on the keyboard, the words will come."

"Wow. Thousands of writers would disagree with you."

He shrugs, drawing my attention to the shifting muscles beneath the worn cotton of his T shirt. "Don't care. I'm not out to win friends."

"I can see that. Living all the way out here, keeping your identity secret." We reach the kitchen and I'm momentarily distracted by the tantalizing aroma of cheese and tomato. "Let me guess. You're a master chef in the kitchen too."

"Buzz is the chef around here and he's damn good."

I want to ask what the deal is between them. There's a

softening in his tone when he talks about Cole and I'm curious.

"Cole's your housekeeper?"

"Unofficially." He puts on oven mitts and slides a baking tray out of the oven, before placing it on the stove top. "We met about five years ago. He needed a place to stay, I had an empty cottage, so he came for a while, started helping out, and never left. He makes a great PA too. We've been best friends ever since."

There's more to that story. I can tell by the tension bunching his shoulders as he dishes the cannelloni onto two plates, but it's not my place to ask. Maintaining civility is imperative if I'm to take advantage of our one-on-one time over the next week.

"I chatted to my best friend this afternoon. Rosie. She's in PR and is good at it."

He glances at me with a raised eyebrow. "Are you trying to pitch me?"

I chuckle. "She asked me to, but I told her with the kind of advances you command, your publicist would eviscerate her."

When he laughs, his face transforms and I feel it like a stab to the gut, and lower. "I hate it when book deals get reported."

"Why? You're an amazing writer, you should command top dollar advances."

He eyeballs me with open speculation. "You're nothing like what I thought you'd be."

"Uh-oh. Dare I ask what you expected?"

He studies me for a second and the intensity of his stare makes me heat up from the inside out. "Someone more jaded. More cynical."

"Why?"

"Your reviews are quite acerbic."

"My reviews are honest."

"Tell that to the authors you DNF."

There's a hint of resentment in his tone and I have no idea where it's coming from. "When I label a book the dreaded Did Not Finish, it's one opinion, as I'm sure everyone knows. As a hopeful author, I'll probably get my fair share of DNF's, if I ever get published, that is. It's part of the territory."

He wants to say more. I can see it in every tense line of his body. "Let's eat, then I want to discuss something with you."

"Should I be worried?"

"Not really."

It's a vague platitude, and as we devour the ridiculously good cannelloni and garlic bread, and sip at an exceptional shiraz that probably costs as much as my monthly wage, I can't help but wonder what he wants to talk to me about.

I'm not sure if it's the sublime wine or a belly full of amazing pasta that lulls me into a false sense of security, but when we stand to clear the table and my foot catches on a chair leg and I stumble, his hand shoots out to steady me and we end up too close.

Close enough I can feel the heat radiating off him.

Close enough I can see his pupils dilate.

Close enough I can smell the fine wine on his breath.

I'm not sure if it's the dating drought I've been in, the half-bottle of wine I've consumed when I barely have more than a glass, or the sheer unadulterated magnetism of this sexy man, but I give in to a shockingly irresponsible impulse.

I kiss him.

Chapter Sixteen

AXEL

One minute I'm struggling to find the words to tell Mia about Adele Lavash, the next her lips are locked on mine and my head explodes.

Turns out, not being with a woman for over five years means I can't think rationally, I can't compute anything, other than the gift of having Mia in my arms.

Her lips are soft, her grip on me hard, as if she's hanging on for dear life. I know the feeling. I'm swamped with sensation: the sinuous tangle of her tongue with mine, the scrape of her fingers down my back, the beguiling fragrance of vanilla with an underlying hint of peach. I'm on overload, torn between sweeping the table clean and laying her on it so I can feast on her, and stopping this kiss before it goes too far.

I must stop it. It's the right thing to do. She's not going to like me very much when I tell her everything and having sex will mess with that, no matter how much I want to.

Certain parts of my anatomy are straining with the urge to

be buried deep inside her and my hands tingle with the impulse to skim every inch of her skin.

But I can't turn off the logical part of my brain; the part insisting that this is wrong on so many levels. I live with enough guilt every day without adding to it.

I ease my lips away from hers with regret, hating that the right thing to do feels so wrong.

She can't look at me. Her gaze is fixed on my throat, and I place my finger under her chin and tip it up. "Hey."

When her eyes reluctantly meet mine, I see equal parts desire and embarrassment. "Can I blame that out of line kiss on the wine?" She winces. "I rarely drink and I'm tired and I don't want to muddy our professional relationship—"

I press a finger to her lips, realizing my mistake a fraction too late when I register how pillowy soft and plump they are from our kiss.

I snatch my finger away as if burned and say, "It's forgotten."

Unlikely, and the blatant skepticism in her eyes screams she doesn't believe me. "I'll help you clean up."

I want to say no and tell her to go to bed, but I need to talk to her about Adele, so I offer a brief nod and head to the sink. I rinse and stack the dishwasher, while she wipes down the countertops and cleans the rest of the kitchen. We work in silence and I wish I'd put music on, anything to drown out the sound of her breathing I've somehow become acutely attuned to.

I can smell her too, that tempting vanilla and peach fragrance, and I wonder if it's her body wash, shampoo, or perfume. But if she's moving around, how can I smell her...I stifle a groan. When she was pressed against me during that kiss, her fragrance must've imprinted on my T-shirt, and I surreptitiously pull the neckline upward and sniff. Yep, it's delectable, and I resist the urge to yank off my T-shirt because I'm befuddled enough.

Why did she kiss me?

I don't buy her drunk excuse because she's moving around the kitchen fine, without a stagger or stumble in sight. Was it a fangirl moment for her, something she can boast to her bestie about? Or am I being a dick and it's a simple matter of chemistry and the underlying physical attraction I've been trying to deny too?

Whatever her rationale, I can't ask her. Best to ignore it, put it down to momentary madness, and move on.

I turn off the taps, start the dishwasher, and swivel to find her staring at me. At my ass, more precisely, and in a second the heat in the kitchen ratchets up.

I expect her to turn away, to pretend that didn't happen, but she drags her gaze upward reluctantly and when our eyes meet, I know I'm in trouble.

"What are you doing?" The question comes out gravelly as my throat seizes when she stalks toward me.

"Being honest with myself."

"Mia..."

I want to warn her off. To say this isn't a good idea. To reiterate all the reasons why we shouldn't do this.

But when she places her palms against my chest, branding me with her heat, and slides them slowly downward, I'm a goner.

"Haven't you ever done something you know is wrong, but you can't resist?" She murmurs against the side of my mouth, before trailing featherlight kisses along my jaw toward my ear. "This is madness, I know. Because I'm not sure if I even like you. But I want you so badly I can't stop."

Her teeth nip my earlobe, earning a guttural groan that feels like it's ripped from deep within me. I'm powerless to stop this even though I should.

"I'm not sure I like you either."

It's a crap thing to say but she chuckles and nips me again, harder this time and on my neck. "In that case, why don't we reenact the classic enemies to lovers trope?"

I bark out a laugh but eyeball her. "Are you sure?"

"I've never been surer of anything." Her fingers toy with the waistband of my jeans and I grit my teeth as a tsunami of lust swamps me and makes me forget everything but my name. "Let's do this."

Chapter Seventeen

MIA

I'm warm. Hot. Burning up. I can't sleep when I'm this hot
and I wonder why I've gone to bed with an extra blanket.
Until I open my eyes and see the weight draped across half of
my body isn't a blanket.

It's Axel Low.

Stunned, I peek at him—the smattering of hair on his arm
flung over me, the muscles of his back delineated, the curve of
his ass—and it all comes flooding back.

Me crushing on him when he spent hours critiquing my
manuscript yesterday.

Rosie's insistence I should do him.

A cozy dinner, the two of us shut off from the outside
world.

Me kissing him.

Me jumping his bones.

The most mind-blowing sex of my life.

I stifle a groan as the full magnitude of what I've done hits me.

I've slept with *the* Axel Low.

The man who's going to help launch my publishing career with a bit of luck.

The man who admitted he doesn't like me—albeit after I said the same to him.

The man who I'm stuck with until the weather gods deem they've dumped enough snow on us.

What the hell have I done?

This isn't good. The situation. Not the sex. The sex was phenomenal. Definitely five stars. If I had to review it, I'd use superlatives like *'outstanding, exciting, unforgettable.'* But I need to extricate myself from his bed pronto and head back to my room so I can process what I'm going to say and how I'm going to act when he wakes up.

I carefully wriggle out from under his arm and do a weird half turn and slide so that I end up on the floor on my knees, almost squashing Mr. Darcy in the process. He gives an annoyed meow and glares at me, and I mouth "sorry, cat," before crawling to where I spy the first part of my clothing on the floor, my bra. I hate to think of the view Axel will get if he wakes now and sees me naked on all fours, but thankfully he slumbers, snoring softly, and I complete my reconnaissance mission to find my clothes in record time.

I'm almost at the door when I see Mr. Darcy has been walking alongside me and I stifle a giggle at the incongruous picture we must make. With a quick glance at the bed to ensure Axel is still sleeping, I arch my back in a cat pose, and hilariously, Mr. Darcy mimics me.

This time I can't stop a chuckle from bubbling up and I stand and make a break for it, grateful for the floor heating as I do a naked dash down the hall to my room. I have no idea what time it is, and after a glance at my cell on the desk I see it's just after two. I'm too wired to sleep so after a quick shower I slip into my PJs—the cute pink ones covered in book stacks—and do the one thing guaranteed to make me fall asleep. Read.

I have several ARCs lined up on my Kindle, but I need the comforting weight of a book in my hands right now, so I head to the library, considering I only brought Axel's books for autographing and I've already reread all of them several times over the years.

The library is illuminated by two lamps, one on his desk, the other on a table beside the sofa, and I slip inside. I could spend a lifetime browsing the countless books on these shelves, but I need something to put me to sleep fast, so I choose the first book my hand lands on.

An Adele Lavash raunch-fest aptly titled Do Me Again.

Considering my complete apathy for her prose, skimming the first few pages will definitely put me to sleep, and I curl up on the sofa with my legs tucked under me and open the first page.

Before I start reading, I lift the book to my nose and inhale deeply, savoring the perfect new paper smell. Nothing grounds me like the smell of a new book and I've been a proud book sniffer since I started reading as a preschooler. Jace teases me incessantly at work when he sees me practically salivate over a new ARC because he knows the first thing I'll do is open it and sniff.

I inhale again, deeper this time, instantly soothed. I lower it, the irony not lost on me that I've picked a book that probably features what I did with Axel a few hours ago and maybe reading erotica and getting hot and bothered isn't conducive to forgetting what happened.

Then again, how raunchy can it get in the first few pages? More than likely I'll be bored and ready to drift off before the end of the first chapter.

I start reading.

Primrose didn't believe in second chances. Her motto was one strike and you're out, so when Matt Larkspur returned to town, all six-foot-four, tanned, muscled, and determined to charm her, she had four words for him.

Not in this lifetime.

Annoyingly, he didn't speak for several long, loaded moments as he stood beneath the oak in the front yard of the house they'd once owned together, his lazy grin doing crazy things to her insides. Damn him.

"What do you want, Matt?"

He took a step forward, another, bringing him within touching distance, and her skin pebbled. "That's easy." His stare bore into her and she resisted the urge to rub her bare arms. "You."

She sensed his intention a second before he reached out and laid a palm over her heart. It bucked and pounded, revealing how much his proximity turned her on. "And I can tell you want me too."

"Enjoying it?"

I jump as Axel sits on the sofa beside me. I can't believe I'd been so caught up in the story I hadn't heard him come in. He's only wearing grey sweatpants and I avert my eyes from all that glorious, tanned chest. A chest I'd explored in detail earlier—every dip, every curve. I swallow; it does little for my dry throat.

"I couldn't sleep," I say, closing the book, my face flushing as I glance at the cover—a bare-chested Adonis with a pretty blonde on her knees, her face at hip level, looking up at him in adoration—and back at Axel. It's silly to be embarrassed caught reading erotica, especially when he stocks it in his library, but hot on the heels of our very own sexploits I'm a tad mortified.

"You didn't answer my question." He points to the book.

"Are you enjoying it?"

Surprisingly, I am. The prose is a vast improvement on the last book I read by the author, where a married couple started having sex with their neighbor on the second page and didn't let up for the first few chapters, which is why I labelled it a DNF. Boring didn't come close to describing that book.

"Actually, I am enjoying it."

"You sound surprised. You're not a fan of erotica?"

The way he says erotica makes my libido sit up and howl. "Not a fan of Adele Lavash."

"Why?"

"Too much sex, not enough plot."

"Nothing wrong with too much sex."

He's eyeballing me with a tempting mix of confusion and daring. Is he asking what I think he's asking? Does he want a repeat?

"Agreed," I say cautiously, in case I misinterpreted.

There's no mistaking what he means when he plucks the book out of my hands, places it on the floor with surprising care, and cups my face with his hands.

"I've never seen anything sexier than you in those pajamas and I want to tear them off."

The blazing desire in his eyes makes me lightheaded and I barely squeak out "okay" before his lips are on mine. Commanding. Demanding. Persuasive in their power to make me lose my mind and give in to be consumed by him again.

Heat floods me as he settles his weight over me and groans something unintelligible in my ear. His tongue flicks my lobe and I arch, every nerve ending in my body straining toward him.

He trails kisses toward my collarbone and my skin erupts in goosebumps when he traces it with his tongue.

I make an embarrassing mewl and he lifts his head, his pupils so large I could drown in them.

"You okay?"

"Never better." I frame his face in my hands and draw him toward me to prove it, nipping his lower lip before sweeping my tongue across it to soothe.

I do it again, harder this time, and I feel him pulse between my legs.

"You know, it's a proven fact grey sweatpants act like an aphrodisiac for most women."

I feel the deep rumble in his chest where it's pressed against mine a moment before he chuckles. "You're kidding."

"I'm not." My breath quickens as I toy with the band of his sweatpants. "Perhaps I need to take them off so you'll believe me?"

The tip of his tongue darts out to moisten his lip and I'm riveted by the action, desperate to mimic it. "Are you trying to get me naked?"

I give the faintest of nods before he rises off me and kneels next to the sofa, his stare determined and passion-hazed as he focuses on the top button of my pajama top. He toys with it, taking an inordinate amount of time to slide it through the hole, and I yelp as his fingertips graze my flushed skin.

"So sensitive," he murmurs, inching down to the next button, and every inch of me is on fire, craving his touch.

"Just get it off," I whisper, eyeballing him so he can see the erotic torture he's putting me through.

His eyes widen in faux innocence. "But I thought you didn't want me to rip them off you?"

I growl in frustration and he captures my lips a second later in a scorching open-mouthed kiss that leaves me light-headed and clinging to him.

Thankfully, he doesn't tear my favorite PJs, but he has them off in record time, his hands and mouth everywhere, teasing me, making me clutch his head as he moves lower...

Chapter Eighteen

AXEL

I knew I kept a blanket on this sofa for a reason. With Mia sated in my arms, her head resting on my shoulder and one of her legs draped across mine, the blanket over the two of us adds to the coziness.

I hadn't intended for this to happen. Again. But the moment I saw her wearing those dorky pajamas, curled up on my library sofa reading, I couldn't help myself. I don't play games, never have, so I blurted the first thing that popped into my head: I wanted to tear those pajamas off her.

I half-expected her to deflect, to pretend like I'd made a joke, so when she gave the go-ahead...I had to have her. And it was just as good as the first time, if not better.

I could attribute the mind-numbing pleasure on the five-year drought for me, but I'm not delusional. Losing my mind has more to do with Mia and her responsiveness than the length of time since I last had sex.

That's another oddity: the damnedest thing happened

after the first time we had sex in my bed.

I slept for five hours straight.

That hasn't happened since Paula's accident, and while it may be the sleep-inducing hormones released after an orgasm, I like to think it was having Mia next to me, warm and soft and pliant, that lulled me into slumber.

Man, the first rousing bout of sex in five years and I turn into a sap. Maybe I should start writing romance too?

"That was...unexpected." Her voice is soft, tentative, and kicks me where I least expect it: my heart.

"Blame those damn pajamas."

She chuckles. "The ones now lying in a heap on the floor?"

"Yeah. I'm a sucker for a fellow nerd. How could I resist?"

She makes a soft pfft sound of outrage because she thinks I'm teasing. I'm not. Those PJs are beyond cute. "I'll have you know those are the height of fashion for book lovers."

"I'll take your word for it." My arms tighten around her, and she glances up at me, her lips within kissing distance, and I struggle not to give in to the urge to do just that. We need to talk, something we should've done before things got this far.

Because I've finally admitted the truth to myself.

Labelling the sex earlier as a one-off had been foolish. What we've just done on this sofa proves it. And I want more. For however long we're snowed in, I want to ravish Mia Samson. My enemy.

At what point did I lose sight of my goal? The first time she called me out on my grumpy BS? When she accepted my critique of her work with grace rather than defensiveness? After the first orgasm?

Whatever has caused my brain fade, I'm not a complete idiot. I no longer see her as someone to be taught a lesson. But I do need her onside and that's going to take some doing once she discovers the truth.

"I want to talk to you about something."

"Uh-oh." She eases out from under my arm and sits up, clutching the blanket to her. "Please don't spoil the best sex I've ever had with excuses or retribution."

I like that she's as blunt as me. "The best, huh?"

She rolls her eyes. "Of course you'd focus on that part."

"Hey, I'm a guy who hasn't had any in five years. Give me a break."

Her lips part in a small, shocked O. "You haven't had sex in five years?"

Sadness and guilt aren't conducive to dating and I haven't missed it. I've been so focused on making enough money to ensure Paula has the best care that I haven't given my lack of sex a second thought. Not that Mia needs to hear it.

"So I'm a monk. Sue me."

"I'm surprised, that's all." Her fingertips skim my chest and I'm semi-erect in an instant. "I mean, look at you."

"I've been busy with my career." I still her exploring fingers with my hand because I can't think when she's touching me and if she keeps this up, I'll never get around to telling her about Adele. "That's what I wanted to talk to you about."

A puzzled frown creases her brow and I feel her body stiffen slightly. "Okay."

"I have a connection with Adele Lavash and for personal reasons, she needs her next book to fly." I point to the book, partially hidden by Mia's pajamas on the floor. "That one's releasing soon, and if you label it another DNF when you review, it could be dire for her."

I don't like the way she's looking at me, like she can see straight through me and isn't happy with what she sees.

"Are you seriously trying to influence me into giving a good review?" Her tone is frigid, colder than the snow falling outside.

"I'm trying to get you to be objective."

It's the wrong thing to say because I've implied she isn't, and she leaps to her feet, wrapping the blanket around her. "Nobody tells me how to review. Ever." She jabs a finger at me. "How would you feel if someone told me how to review your books?"

Before I can answer, she rushes on, "You'd hate it. Because it shows bias."

I need to defuse this situation before it gets out of hand and I blow it completely. "I'm not telling you how to review. I'm just trying to get you to see that Adele needs a break with this next book and your opinion holds sway in the reading community, so perhaps you can take it easy on her."

Her eyes widen and she takes a step back. "I'm such an idiot. She means something to you, doesn't she?"

I can't lie, so I nod, and her face hardens into a stoic mask.

"What you just said, about you not having sex for the last five years, is crap, isn't it?" She shakes her head, tousled strands falling on her shoulders. "You're sleeping with her—"

"I'm not. She's—"

"Stop." She holds up her hand, her eyes narrow, her stare accusing. "I don't want to hear any more."

With surprising elegance, she sweeps up her pajamas off the floor and tucks the blanket around her tighter, like a queen in a toga.

I stand, a big mistake considering the evidence of how magnificent I find her even when she's riled is tenting the front of my sweatpants.

Her imperious glance sweeps over me, lingers on my groin for a second, before her upper lip curls in a sneer before she turns away and strides toward the door.

"Mia, please, let me explain..."

She slams the door on her way out.

Chapter Nineteen

MIA

Who knew having amazing sex with a world-famous author you've been fan-girling over forever makes you irrational?

Because that's exactly what I'd been a few moments ago, accusing Axel of sleeping with Adele Lavash, behaving like a jealous harpy, going a little crazy...ugh. Beyond embarrassing.

His timing could've been better—asking me about work while I was naked in his arms sucked—but technically, he hadn't done anything wrong. Whether he has a personal relationship with Adele or not, it's irrelevant, because I wanted to have sex with him and I'd instigated it. This is on me.

I cringe at the memory of my overreaction. How on earth had I jumped to conclusions, equating his request for me to go easy on Adele's book with sleeping with her?

I'm not an unreasonable person usually. I saw enough of Mom's foolish theatrics whenever one of her boyfriends dumped her and I vowed to never be like that. No man was worth embarrassing yourself over. Yet that's exactly what I'd done a few minutes ago; with a guy who has the power to help my career, no less.

A chill makes me shiver and I wrap the blanket tighter around me. I have no idea how I'm going to face Axel again. Hopefully, when the sun comes up in a few hours—if it peeks through the blizzard that is, which is highly unlikely considering the snow hasn't subsided—it'll cast a new light on the mess I made, and we can behave like civilized humans. Though technically that only applies to me, as he wasn't the one ranting like a lunatic.

The kicker is, I wasn't so outraged by him asking to cut Adele a break, it was the way he'd said it, like she meant something to him. And hot on the heels of another incredible bout of sex, some jealous imp I didn't know resided inside me had snapped. Mortifying.

To add insult to injury, Mr. Darcy has followed me into my room before I could shut the door and is now perched on my desk, staring at me with those knowing golden eyes, like he knows I've screwed up and finds me distinctly lacking in brain cells.

"What are you looking at?" I scowl and head for the bathroom, where I have a quick wash before slipping into my pajamas. I'll never be able to wear the darn things again without the memory of Axel saying he wanted to tear them off me reminding me of this crazy interlude we shared.

I'm a living trope. Snowed in with a sexy stranger. Forced proximity. Grumpy sunshine—no prizes for guessing he's the grump and I'm the sunshine in this scenario. Enemies to lovers. It's all so trite and I wouldn't believe it if I'm not living it right now.

I'm so discombobulated I do the one thing guaranteed to distract.

I write.

In my post-coital haze earlier, I'd contemplated diving

back into my regency romance. Now, I open my thriller without hesitation and channel every ounce of frustration into torturing the victim: picturing Axel the entire time.

I'm a slow writer. I usually try thirty-minute sprints to bump up my word count, but my output rarely exceeds two thousand words during four sprints. Now, I can't stop. My fingers tap at the keyboard with increasing speed until I glance at the time, almost five a.m., and can't believe I've written 3541 words in two hours.

Exhilarated, I make sure I've saved my work and emailed a copy to myself, before closing my laptop. My eyes are gritty with fatigue, my neck is sore, my wrists twang, but I don't care. I can snatch a few more hours sleep now. The longer the better, so I don't have to see Axel.

Childish, because we're going to run into each other eventually. Forced proximity, remember? But I'm sure I'll function better after some sleep.

Mr. Darcy is curled up at the foot of my bed and I don't have the heart to dislodge him, so I slip under the covers. Sleep is elusive as I rehash every moment of my time with Axel. The good and the bad. I may want to get an intro into the publishing industry from one of the best, but now, the snow can't stop falling quick enough.

I need to escape.

Chapter Twenty

AXEL

I've never been articulate. At school, I was the quiet kid with his nose in a book who got teased. That eased in high school because I was half decent at basketball and it didn't matter so much that I didn't speak a lot, I let my three-pointers do the talking. Once I started working on job sites, the sound of power tools drowned out any speech so talking was irrelevant. These days, I say what I need to say via writing and that's enough for me.

But considering the way I botched things with Mia in the wee small hours, hiding away for the last five years and not conversing with many people beyond Buzz, the staff at Sunny Pines, and Paula, hasn't done me any favors.

I didn't sleep after she stormed out of the library. I'd contemplated going after her for a few seconds before realizing I'd only make things worse, so I picked up Adele's upcoming release and started reading. I tried to be as objective as possible, to nitpick any reason Mia might have to disparage it. But I have to admit, it's one of her best.

Mia hadn't been wrong in saying the early Lavash books had been all sex and little plot. I know that's what had been selling at the time and she'd ridden a huge wave of success by giving readers what they wanted and writing to trend. But that's the thing about trends, they can become outdated in an instant, and the literary world had turned to women's fiction and historicals more recently, leaving Adele Lavash's sales on a downward trajectory—and that's before Mia had marked her last book as a DNF.

I know I can help Mia see sense when she reviews Do Me Again. It's not like I'm asking her to give it a rave. But this book needs to sell and all I want is for Mia not to hamper those sales with one of her scathing reviews; or another dreaded DNF.

I'm not an ostrich. I don't stick my head in the sand. I read reviews of my books. I can't help it. It's a way for me to keep abreast of what readers are thinking. And some are less than complimentary, with some of the worst being *'he keeps churning out this drivel', 'I may have thrown up in my mouth a little due to the cheesiness of the detective work,' 'how can any self-respecting editor let this crap be published'.*

But for every one star review I'm lucky enough to get many more five stars, so it balances in my favor. I know I'm not invincible though. I'm only as good as my last book. And Chrissie wouldn't have insisted I host this ridiculous writing retreat unless the publisher is seriously disgruntled with my sales and the effect my lack of media presence is having.

It's not like my virtual assistant doesn't post daily on a few social media sites: writing quotes mostly, generic book pictures, glowing reviews, my covers posed on desks, photos of libraries around the world. But readers value the personal touch and not knowing what I look like, where I live, and what I eat for breakfast is apparently a big deal in this age where bestselling authors are treated like minor celebs and fans are hungry for more.

Chrissie has emailed me asking for an update on how the retreat is going because she's heard about the 'inclement weather.' Understatement of the year, considering I've never seen a blizzard like this in my lifetime and who knows how long I'll be snowed in with Mia Samson.

As for how things are going...I hope Mia managed to get some sleep and is ready to listen to reason when we see each other shortly. I'm aware my timing could've been better. Asking her for a favor regarding Adele's next book just after we'd had sex probably wasn't the smartest idea. I should've waited, but I'd been so intent on doing the right thing and letting her know my intentions rather than sleeping with her again and muddying our relationship further that I'd screwed up.

Though her anger had surprised me. She'd taken it as a personal affront, like I'd asked her to doctor a review rather than try to be objective. As for accusing me of lying about my celibacy the last five years and sleeping with Adele...it had been outlandish.

But we've all done crazy things in the spur of the moment, and I won't hold it against her. We're snowed in for the foreseeable future and I need to make an effort to get our relationship back on track, otherwise she won't take my request seriously and I can't afford to have Adele's next book tank.

Mia hasn't come out of her room yet and it's after ten, so I'm assuming hunger will tempt her toward the kitchen eventually.

Buzz has tried calling too but the voice message is too garbled due to static. I should call him back and hope the line is bad again so he can't hear how sleep-deprived and out of sorts I am. He can read me like a book, bad pun intended.

I bring up my favorites on my cell and tap his name. The dial tone is faint and I'm about to disconnect when he answers.

"Axel, that you?"

"No, it's your long-lost fairy godmother."

He chuckles. "I see being snowed in hasn't improved your lousy sense of humor."

"That's because there's nothing remotely funny about being stuck here."

"I thought you'd be in heaven, having someone like Mia to keep you company."

I snort and swipe my other hand over my face. Yeah, like that will dislodge memories of Mia and what we did. The soft moans she makes when I kiss her stomach, the groans when I nibble on her neck, the blush that stains her chest when she's on the verge of coming.

"What does that mean, someone like Mia?"

"Sweet. Sassy. Female. Human."

I need to get off the topic of Mia before I blurt exactly how amazing I've found being stuck with Mia. "Speaking of human, your non-human friend is fine."

"Of course he is. I know you love Mr. Darcy. You just pretend not to."

"I'm not pretending. I hate cats."

"Hate. Love. It's all interchangeable." Buzz sniggers. "Do you hate Mia?"

He's relentless and I know I'll have to give him something to get Buzz off my case. "Mia is fine. We got some work done yesterday afternoon."

"All work and no play?"

There was plenty of play, but Buzz doesn't need to know that. "Where are you?"

"At the Sugar Plum Inn. None of the other retreat attendees made it before flights into Omaha were grounded, so I guess that's one good thing."

Ironic, that in inviting Mia here earlier than the others, I'd inadvertently ensured we'd be stuck together. If she wasn't here, would I be pounding away at my keyboard, enjoying the luxury of no contact with anybody, and writing as many words as humanly possible? A moot point, with her proving more of a distraction than I could've anticipated.

"At least you have enough food for the two of you, considering we stocked up for all those extra people."

"Yeah," I say, the mention of food making me think of dinner last night and that kiss that led to more.

"What's going on, bud?"

I grip the cell tighter. Of course Buzz has caught on that something's wrong. He has a knack for it and holds me accountable even when I don't want to be. "Nothing. Why?"

"Your tone is off."

"It's the cell reception."

There's a long pause and I glance at the screen, expecting we've been disconnected. But Buzz is still there because I hear a heavy sigh of disapproval.

"What have you done? Not everyone tolerates your antisocial personality like I do and if you've pissed off Mia, she might trash your next book—"

"I slept with her."

Buzz pauses for all of two seconds before letting out a loud whoop. "About time you got some. I'm surprised you haven't sustained a wrist injury all these years, and not from repetitive strain on the keyboard."

"Prick," I mutter, and Buzz laughs.

"Well, I guess you don't mind being snowed in after all."

"I mind," I mutter, pinching the bridge of my nose to stave off the hint of a headache. "You know I value my solitude."

"Uh-oh. Was it bad? Were you no good? Have you forgotten how?"

"I did just fine." Better than fine. Stupendous doesn't come close to describing sex with Mia. "But we're butting heads over a few professional issues so that needs to be resolved."

"Don't screw this up, doofus. You need to—"

I have no idea if he's referring to sleeping with Mia or working with her, and luckily, the telecommunication company's dodgy blizzard reception chooses that moment to disconnect our call before he can give me any unsolicited advice.

Though I can't help but wonder what Buzz had been about to say. *'You need to lighten up? You need to cut her some slack? You need to get a life?'*

All of them could apply but right now, I need to make a start on smoothing things over with Mia, and that involves presenting her with my go-to comfort breakfast.

Chapter Twenty-One

MIA

I'm not a morning person. Never have been. I need to inhale a minimum of two cups of tea to function like a human, but today that involves leaving the sanctity of my room and risking a potential run-in with Axel.

Silly, because I'm going to have to face him eventually, but after a few hours' sleep, when I usually need six hours at least, I'm extra grumpy.

I peek out the window, to find a winter wonderland. Pristine white as far as I can see. It's beautiful and nothing like the snow in Manhattan which turns dirty and murky all too fast. I've always been a city girl so have only seen this kind of snow in the movies. The prettiness of it beckons and I wonder if I can sneak outside to make my first snow angel ever; one of the mundane things most people take for granted but I've never done.

One of my earliest childhood memories is of Dad

promising to take me snowboarding. I'd been about four and Mom chastised him, saying I was too young. Dad disagreed but sadly, we never got to do our snow trip because he died of a heart attack two weeks later. Mom had been inconsolable, until a mere eight months later when she invited a 'friend' over for dinner, one of the guys she worked with. I'd been a brat because I didn't like the way she looked at him; with a smile she used to reserve for my dad when he teased her.

Unfortunately, that had been the start of my mother trying to assuage her grief with an endless string of boyfriends. None of them were keepers. Mom attracted losers: guys who couldn't hold down a job, guys looking for a place to stay, married guys.

I could never understand how I could take one look at a guy and pick his type, but Mom couldn't. Unless she didn't care and needed a man around because she couldn't stand the loneliness. Whatever her motivation, the losers kept on coming and as I grew older and caught them leering at me, I learned to avoid home and the local library became my sanctuary.

I also learned to rarely trust men because most of them break your heart.

My stomach rumbles and I acknowledge any snow play will have to wait. I need sustenance and caffeine. Without a side of Axel.

I slip into jeans and a T-shirt, grateful for the incredible central heating. I could be stuck in worse places, but with a better companion.

I open my door slowly and peek up and down the hallway before leaving my room. I'm like a thief, slinking toward the kitchen, on high alert for any Axel sightings. But he's nowhere to be seen, until I make a beeline for the kettle, and I hear a throat clearing behind me.

"Good morning."

His greeting washes over me, his deep voice as appealing as the rest of him, and my hormones, the ones that are trained on him, snap to attention.

"Is it?" I mutter under my breath, before turning to face him, only to find the table has been set, with a plate of pancakes in the middle surrounded by caramelized bananas, fresh strawberries, and a jug of maple syrup. I salivate a little. "Did you make those?"

It's a stupid, inane question, considering there's no one else here and he nods. "Writers needs to feed their muse, even if I don't believe in them."

"You don't have a muse?"

He shakes his head. "I believe in hard work and persistence earning rewards."

I want to argue the point, because I'm a firm believer creativity springs from a deep inner well we need to nourish, but he's making an effort and I don't want to pick up where we left off. "Do you eat like this every day?"

"Hell no. A quick smoothie is more my style."

"So is all this for me?"

"Yeah, a peace offering." He's shamefaced. "I didn't like how we left things during the night and I'm hoping you'll give me a chance to explain after breakfast."

He's conciliatory when I'm the one who should be apologizing and the thought of how I overreacted in the library makes me inwardly cringe.

"Actually, I was way out of line with all that stuff I said. Completely irrational." I screw up my nose. "No idea what came over me."

He looks like he wants to say more, before he gives a little shake of his head. "Coffee?"

"I don't drink the stuff, but I'd love a gallon of tea, please."

I sit and take a strawberry, popping it into my mouth. "Anything I can do?"

"No, all good thanks."

I watch him fill a mug with coffee from an espresso machine and make my tea, hating the strange fluttering in my chest. I rarely have crushes on guys—I'm too pragmatic—but something about this man has captivated me against my better judgment.

Discounting our mutual love of books and writing—and the sizzling sex—I shouldn't like him. I prefer my men uncomplicated, whereas Axel is the antithesis of that. If I had to use one word to describe him, it would be dour. Yet he has hidden depths and that's what fascinates me. I want to know more when I shouldn't.

He brings our mugs to the table, before sitting opposite me. "Were you writing in the wee small hours?"

"Yeah, how did you know?"

He hesitates, staring into his coffee, before saying, "I came past your room and heard you typing."

I want to ask why he came to my room, but maybe I won't like the answer. Did he want to tell me about his involvement with Adele Lavash or something else, like how I behaved like a crazy person and I should get a grip?

"I was in the zone and the words poured out. Haven't been on a roll like that for ages."

Try never. I like to think my anger at Axel potentially using me when he has a thing for Adele Lavash fueled my word count in the early hours of the morning, but deep down I know differently. It had been the way he made me come alive with every caress, every stroke, every kiss, that made my fingers fly across the keyboard. I've never been so inspired.

"It's magic when that happens." He sips at his coffee, his eyes surprisingly clear for someone who had a madwoman accuse of him sleeping with Adele Lavash last night when I had no right to. "I love that buzz when I lose track of time because I'm so immersed in the story, then I look at the clock and hours have flown by in what seems like minutes."

I'm mesmerized by his animated expression when he talks about writing. He's like a different person. The tiny dent between his brows vanishes and he talks with his hands, like he can't get the words out fast enough. It's incredibly sexy. Or that could be the memory of his shifting expressions last night: the reverence when his gaze swept over my naked body, the focus as he pleasured me, the abandon as he thrust into me.

My body is on fire, and I take a gulp of tea; ineffectual to cool me down, but the caffeine might short-circuit my brain into gear.

"Hope you like pancakes," he says, sounding oddly vulnerable as he gestures at the stack between us. "It's my go-to breakfast when I need a pick-me-up."

I dare not ask why he needs a pick-me-up. Self-explanatory, after he had a banshee screeching at him in the middle of the night.

I've never been a jealous person—discounting the tiny green-eyed monster that flares to life when a debut author lands a massive six-figure advance then proceeds to hit the New York Times bestseller list during release week. But professional jealousy is far different to what I experienced last night and it's making me edgy. Having sex with Axel Low does not give me the right to behave like a possessive girlfriend and that's exactly what I did. I need to apologize, but he mentioned wanting to talk after breakfast, and I am ravenous, so I'll eat first, grovel later.

"I love pancakes." I flash him a grateful smile and his gaze lingers on my mouth a tad too long, eliciting more memories: how his lips felt pressed against mine, how he nipped my lip in tiny teasing nibbles, how his tongue swept over it to soothe, how I'd returned the favor.

When he raises an eyebrow, like he can see exactly what I'm thinking reflected in my eyes, I quickly lower my gaze and focus on forking two pancakes onto my plate, spooning caramelized banana over them, and drenching the lot in maple syrup. The weird thing is, I was starving before I entered the kitchen, but with a sexily disheveled Axel sitting across from me—casually mussed hair, stubble-covered jaw, navy T-shirt with flour spatters—my appetite has waned. But eating will give me something to focus on and I desperately need that when I feel his curious gaze on me.

"Have you seen Mr. Darcy?"

I nod. "He's asleep on my bed."

His eyebrows shoot up. "He never does that. He won't even sleep on Buzz's bed."

"Well, he made himself comfortable when I went to bed around five and hasn't budged."

He's staring at me like I've wielded a magic wand.

"What?" I ask, and he shakes his head.

"You're full of surprises."

"I haven't done anything. No idea why that cat's drawn to me when I don't like him at all."

"Don't let Buzz hear you say that. He treats that cat like a king."

"Lucky he isn't here then." It's a flippant remark, but it makes me wonder when this snow will let up. I checked the weather forecast on my cell when I woke but it didn't tell me much other than more snow is predicted. "Any idea when this blizzard will stop?"

The corners of his mouth kick up. "Why? Can't get away fast enough, huh?"

"Something like that." I smile back at him. "Seriously. Will it be much longer?"

"Do I look like a meteorologist?"

No, he looks like the sexiest guy I've ever met, but thankfully I keep that to myself.

"Worried that you'll miss work?"

"Something like that. I've only taken a week off." Not that it's a big deal. I can read here and submit my reviews remotely. But that's not what I'm concerned about. Being stuck for longer than seven days with Axel will give my crush time to bloom and I can't have that happening. "It's just that I've never been to Nebraska and have no idea if this blizzard will continue for another day or a month."

"It can't last thirty days," he mutters, looking so pained I can't help but laugh.

"That would mean I'll definitely outstay my welcome."

His rueful chuckle warms me better than the tea as I take another sip. "I value my peace and quiet."

"And I'm a disruptive influence?"

"Something like that." He eyeballs me, daring me to remember exactly how much I disrupted—or should that be corrupted?—him last night.

Not that I need the encouragement. I'm doing enough remembering on my own, thank you very much. And the longer he sits across from me, staring at me like he's replaying every erotic detail in his mind, makes it tougher for me not to instigate a repeat, hunger be damned.

To prevent from saying anything incriminating, I break off a chunk of pancake with my fork, stab at a piece of banana, and sweep it through a puddle of maple syrup, before stuffing it into my mouth. The sweetness of the syrup and the banana combine perfectly with the fluffiness of the pancake, and I can't prevent an embarrassing little moan slipping out.

I glance up to find Axel watching me, desire darkening his eyes, and I have a hard time swallowing.

"Good?" His tone is low, gravelly, and I'm instantly transported back to last night when he asked the same thing while kissing his way up my thigh.

"Uh-huh," I murmur, my fork poised midway between my plate and mouth, as I try to look away and can't. It's like he's trying to convey a message I have no hope of interpreting; or maybe I don't want to.

Because I know once I lower my guard again around this guy, I'm a goner.

Chapter Twenty-Two

AXEL

I thought sleeping with Mia would get my unexpected infatuation out of my system. Turns out, not so much.

Breakfast was sheer torture.

The appreciative sounds she made while eating the pancakes...I was rock-hard the entire time. I guess I should be happy. Cooking her Paula's pancakes—my sister swore that adding lemon zest to the batter took them to the next level and she was right—had achieved my main goal, to get us back on even footing. But having Mia smiling at me again makes me want her even more and I have no idea what to do.

There's no question that while she's stuck here, I want Mia. Sex that good needs to be repeated. But it's going to muddy our professional relationship once the truth comes out and I can't afford to have her disparage my novels like she did Adele's.

Though maybe I'm being unfair, and she won't take her

personal dislike of me out on my books when she learns everything.

Yeah, and I'm about to win a Booker. No way, no how.

Telling her a little about Adele will be a good test to see how she'll react to the rest. Her irrational jealousy last night had surprised me, but it means what happened between us is more than just sex and I'm okay with that. I've never been a big fan of one-night stands and have dated the women I've slept with. Though considering I knew Mia for all of one day before sleeping with her makes a mockery of that. Feelings are irrelevant here. It's not like we don't have an expiration date. As long as she knows what I want and it won't complicate matters, why shouldn't we indulge in a short-term fling?

"What are you thinking about?"

I've been gazing out the window while contemplating how much to tell her and I turn to find her curled up on the sofa like Mr. Darcy, her legs tucked under her and her smile smug, like she can read my thoughts.

I can deflect, change the subject, or outright lie, but what's the point when she'll be leaving sooner rather than later once the snow clears or her week's retreat ends, whichever comes first.

I settle for the truth. "I'm thinking about us."

"Us?" It comes out a squeak and I laugh.

"Us. As in you and me." I cross the living room to sit beside her, tempted to reach out and take hold of her foot but needing a clear head to say what needs to be said before I touch her. "Are we going to pretend like that amazing sex didn't happen or are we going to be grown-ups and do it again?" I lower my voice and lean in a little. "And again, and again."

Her eyes widen and her tongue darts out to lick her bottom lip, an innocuous action that shoots straight to my groin. "Is that what you want?"

"Yes. I'm not going to pretend the stupendous sex didn't happen or hedge around it. It was great and for however how long you're here, why stop doing something that feels so good?"

She must like my bluntness because I glimpse admiration in her eyes. "So we're adding another trope to our forced proximity, grumpy sunshine, enemies to lovers thing, are we?"

I tap my temple, pretending to think. "Is short-term fling a trope?"

"It should be, because I like tropes." She pauses, a faint pink staining her cheeks. "Especially that one."

My heart leaps. "Is that a yes?"

She nods and I'm on her, pinning her against the sofa with my body, my hands tangling in her hair, my lips ravishing hers. I taste the faint sweetness of maple syrup as my tongue sweeps into her mouth and she moans as I massage her scalp with my fingertips.

I've never been a sensory person but everything about Mia makes me want to touch and feel and taste and smell. She's addictive.

"You taste yummy," she whispers when we come up for air, and I smile.

"I was thinking the same about you."

She traces my mouth with a fingertip, her expression intense, like she's trying to memorize me. "Should I add that to the list of things we have in common?"

I want to say yes. I like that we've gelled so quickly when I rarely like anybody. But this thing between us has an expiration date and no good can come of making it more than it is. Amazing sex between two compatible people.

"Let's focus on the best thing we have in common." This time when I press my lips to hers it's soft, sensual, before I trail kisses along her jawline, nibble her chin, before claiming her mouth again.

I want to take things slow, to savor her, but when she settles under me and opens her legs to wrap them around me, the air seeps from my lungs.

Our gazes lock and I'm surprised by the hint of vulnerability I glimpse in hers. "Everything okay?"

I cup her cheek, the scattering of goosebumps across her skin indicative that my touch affects her as much as she affects me.

"Everything's great," she murmurs, her lips curving into a smile that's pure wickedness. "Just enjoying the due diligence we're giving to researching the enemies to lovers trope."

"But aren't we suspense writers?"

She nuzzles my neck, her tongue lapping at me like she can't get enough. "It never hurts to be well versed in all genres."

I laugh, surprised by our banter when I'm rock-hard and straining to be inside her. I've never experienced this playfulness during sex before and it's intoxicating. I'm ornery at the best of times and rarely relax, but something about Mia is coaxing me out of my shell and I'm not sure whether to be relieved or scared.

She's making me *feel*, when I haven't in a long time.

"You've gone quiet," she says, scraping her palms over my chest, her grin mischievous when she tweaks my nipples and I let out a groan. "Maybe that's a good thing?"

It is, because I can't think of anything to say, other than how freaking wonderful it is to be given this unexpected gift. Mia is the light to my darkness, the balm to my melancholy, and I want to savor every single moment.

Besides, words are superfluous when she's touching me. I focus on the heat scorching me from the inside out, the tingles rippling over my skin, the pounding of blood in my veins.

Her hands slide around to my back, where she starts

stroking me in long, languid caresses that make every part of me, bar one, melt.

"I love how you feel," she murmurs, surging up to claim my mouth at the same time she digs her nails into my back, and I feel the jolt like an electrocution.

"Hang on," I say, flipping her so she's astride me, and I sit up, so she's straddling me. I want to see her. To feast my eyes on her. To imprint her on my memory.

With her hair mussed, her cheeks flushed, and her lips parted, she's magnificent.

"Axel..." she whispers, and the sound of my name falling from her lips makes me lose control.

Like our previous two encounters, we combust in an explosion of heat and need and passion. It's unlike anything I've experienced with a woman before and I gladly lose my mind, only remembering much later, after she's snug in my arms, that I haven't told her about Adele.

Chapter Twenty-Three

MIA

I could get used to this. A bout of rousing mid-morning sex, followed by two hours of writing alongside one of the most successful thriller authors in the world. I'm not sure if the sex inspired me, or sitting alongside Axel has, but once again my word count is accelerating, over four thousand words in two hours.

I'm finding it increasingly difficult to scatter red herrings throughout my suspense story but I'm taking his advice and just getting the words down, not worrying about re-reading what I've already written or editing of any kind. It's freeing to write this way, getting a first draft done as fast as possible. Until now, I've been obsessively editing every chapter as I go and it's time-consuming.

I did it for the first three chapters because I wanted the partial to shine and earn me a place here. But now I'm lucky enough to have Axel Low giving me firsthand writing advice, I'd be a fool not to listen.

As I end the chapter on a hook, ensuring the reader will want to turn the page, I interlock my fingers and stretch overhead. One of the joints in my neck makes a loud pop and only then does Axel lift his head. He's been so focused on his laptop screen, his fingers tapping so fast on the keyboard, that it's kind of awe-inspiring. Landing this opportunity is a dream come true; and that's before the incredible sex. Though I can't think about that because it's taking all my willpower not to clamber all over him right now.

"Are you okay?" He asks, his eyes sporting that slightly glazed sheen from staring at a computer screen too long before he blinks several times.

"Never better." I point to my laptop. "I've just written four thousand words, a new record for me in two hours."

"That's great." He glances at the word counter in the lower right-hand corner of his manuscript and his eyebrows rise. "I'm usually fast but wow, I've done over six."

I groan. "How is it humanly possible to write more than three thousand words an hour?"

"Practice, and my secret weapon."

"What is it—"

He covers my mouth with his in a scorching kiss that makes me melt against him. "It's you, in case you were wondering," he murmurs when we ease apart. "You inspire me."

My heart expands and struggles to escape my chest, ready to leap into the palm of his hand. Does he have any idea how I feel when he says stuff like that? When he looks at me with a beguiling mix of awe and reverence?

I can't be his inspiration. I can't let my hopes escalate that this brief interlude may mean as much to him as it does to me. And I certainly can't allow emotions to cloud what needs to be a purely physical fling.

I deflect with a glib response. "But you're writing a thriller, not a romance."

A strange expression crosses his face at my flippant answer, but my comment has brought up a topic I've wanted to discuss from last night and would have, if we hadn't got distracted this morning.

"Speaking of romance, I want to apologize for my behavior last night. I know we touched on it earlier but I over-reacted when you said you had a connection with Adele Lavash and I jumped to conclusions." I lay my hand on his thigh. "I'm sorry. I guess I went a little nuts when you told me to take it easy on her next book, because I don't like being told how to do my job." I grimace, knowing if I've come this far, I need to be completely honest. "And I hate that someone who churns out books with little substance is earning fifty times what I do."

His expression is grave, and I second guess the wisdom of revealing so much. But I respect this man's honesty—how he broached the subject of us having a fling earlier was ballsy—and owe him the same courtesy.

"I could take affront on Adele's behalf at several things you just said, such as churning out books with little substance, but I appreciate you admitting your bias stems from profes-sional jealousy."

"I'm not biased," I mutter, and remove my hand from his leg. But he doesn't let me get away with it because he snags my hand and intertwines his fingers with mine.

"Is it all romance in general you have a problem with, or just Adele's?"

Now's my chance to admit I'm writing a regency romance and how much I fell in love with the genre after binge-watching Bridgerton, then obsessively reading the entire series of books.

But I want to make a name for myself in suspense and I

know getting published in one genre is going to be hard enough without muddying the waters with another. Romance is unfairly disparaged by so many critics and readers I don't want to sabotage my chances before I've barely begun.

Axel is a renowned thriller author and I'd be a fool not to take advantage of what he can offer in the way of advice and connections. Bringing my secret passion for regency romance into the equation at this stage would be career suicide.

"I don't have a problem with romance." I send a pointed glare at our joined hands. "See?"

His lopsided smile makes my chest constrict. "How much of Do Me Again did you read yesterday?"

This I can do. Give my honest opinion about a book I've read. "Enough to know it's her best compared with the ones I've read before."

"Why? What's different?"

"The tension. The prose. It's tighter than her last book." I wrinkle my nose. "Having a married couple reconnect sexually by having a threesome with their pervy neighbor doesn't make for a page-turner. The sex became repetitive after a while and that's why I didn't finish it. And her reverse harem books before that got too repetitive. One girl having three guys pant after her when it's hard enough finding one in the real world is too unbelievable. And I know it's a fantasy not remotely based in reality but readers like to identify with characters even while they're reading for escapism."

It seems like he's hanging on my every word, so I swallow the burgeoning lump of resentment in my throat and say, "Adele really means something to you, doesn't she?"

He hesitates for the barest second before nodding. "She has a lot of financial obligations, so the success of her books and the resultant royalties are all-important."

"And that's all?" I know I shouldn't push when in all probability I won't like the answers, but it'll bug me if I don't.

"I mean, you wouldn't ask me to go easy on Do Me Again if you didn't care about her."

His evasiveness is palpable and my heart sinks. "I do care, because I can identify."

I have no idea what that means and before I can ask, he says, "Do you have any siblings?"

"No, only child. Probably better that way, considering my mom could barely raise me."

"You're not close?"

I shake my head, not trusting myself to speak in case he hears the bitterness bound to lace every word I utter when it comes to my mother. I resent the way she barely grieved my dad before moving on, I resent the way she put all her boyfriends ahead of me, and most of all, I resent the way she acts like she's the wounded party in our fractured relationship.

I try not to let it bother me most days. I lead a full life. I have friends and job satisfaction and now, a creative outlet. I'm living the dream. But I'd be lying if I didn't admit to envying the close bond Rosie has with her mom: their spa days, clothes shopping, high teas.

Quashing my antipathy toward my mother, I ask, "What about you? Do you have siblings?"

He hasn't mentioned family in his website bio, and I couldn't find anything online when I researched him before coming.

His jaw clenches and a tiny vein pulses at his temple. "You know everything we discuss during your time here is covered by the non-disclosure agreement, right?"

Surprised by his somberness, I nod.

"Because nobody knows what I'm about to tell you and I want to keep it that way."

I'm not sure whether to be thrilled he trusts me enough to confide in me or disappointed that he thinks so little of me he had to bring up the NDA.

"I have a sister, two years younger than me. She lives in Connecticut."

"Are you two close?"

"Very." His lips compress and he glances away, but not before I see genuine pain in his eyes. "She was in an accident about five years ago and has an acquired brain injury."

I hear the emotion in his strangled tone and squeeze his hand, glad our fingers are still interlinked. "I'm sorry to hear that."

"She's in the best facility money can buy. It's the least I can do after…"

I want to prompt him to finish that sentence, but his expression is so bleak it doesn't seem right I pry.

"She's lucky to have a brother who cares about her." It sounds trite but I mean it. I would've given anything to have a sibling growing up, someone to trust and confide in when Mom wasn't around because she had yet another date. "What about your parents?"

"It's been Paula and me for a while now. Mom died unexpectedly when I was eighteen, Dad a few months later."

He doesn't say how they died; he doesn't have to. I can see how much their deaths must've affected him by the sorrow in his eyes, resulting in an eighteen-year-old teen entrusted with caring for his younger sister. That would breed a special kind of closeness.

We lapse into silence, and I stare at our joined hands, hoping I can convey some level of compassion. It's obvious he loves his sister and somehow blames himself for her accident, but despite wanting to know more I don't ask.

There's a vast difference between a short-term fling and delving into his private life, and I'm crushing enough on this guy without learning what makes him tick.

At least he's not physically involved with Adele Lavash, and I feel foolish all over again for jumping to conclusions.

He's looking so morose I need to distract him, and I know just the way to do it.

I lift our hands to my mouth and press a soft kiss on the back of his.

Our eyes meet and I know I've done the right thing when his clear and he leans toward me.

"If you're trying to distract me, it's working," he murmurs, a moment before his lips brush mine in a butterfly-light kiss that makes me boneless.

He cups my cheek with his free hand and stares into my eyes, and in that moment, I know I'm delusional.

I hate insta-love in romance novels because I don't believe in it, but the tenderness in Axel's gaze undoes me and I'm in danger of reading more into this fling than is good for me.

Chapter Twenty-Four

AXEL

Mia is making cute snuffling sounds in her sleep, and I carefully cover her with the blanket and leave her to slumber. The sofa is comfortable enough she won't wake with a crick in her neck. Besides, considering I heard her tapping away at her keyboard until five this morning, she needs a nap. I do too, but I'm expecting an email from Chrissie about a possible foreign rights sale in Germany for my last book and I need to see if the deal has gone through.

I know it's a bad habit, compulsively checking my inbox, but I can't break it. Ever since I received that first email from Chrissie a decade ago with AUCTION in the subject line, I like to think good things happen via email.

Back then, each email Chrissie sent had been better than the last. She wouldn't write anything in the actual body of the email, she'd just put the highest current bid in the subject header. I watched those numbers start at twenty thousand, jump to fifty, one hundred, two hundred, then a whopping two hundred and fifty thousand. I could scarcely believe Rolf Shelville, who edited greats I could only aspire to be like, wanted to pay that much for my first book. It had been a dream come true.

Paula had been just as excited, and we'd gone out to celebrate the night I inked that deal. I still wonder how different things could've been if we'd decided to stay in that night or gone to a bar three blocks further from my grungy apartment in Venice Beach.

Instead, we'd chosen to have drinks in the dive bar on the next block, and that's the night Paula had met Billie Adams and her life had been irrevocably changed.

I hate myself for subduing the flicker of doubt I had about Billie from the start. No guy is that charming from the get-go, but he'd seemed nice enough and Paula glowed in his presence. He'd even bought me a celebratory tequila shot that night. I haven't been able to touch the stuff since.

A year later, Paula had been admitted to hospital with a fractured pelvis, her left arm smashed in two places, and five broken ribs, from being shoved down the stairs by Billie. It was the first time I learned of his abuse, and I cried so hard that night I almost passed out.

While I'd been high on my self-importance as a soon to be famous author—Rolf had fast tracked my manuscript to be published eighteen months after I signed the contract—working with my assigned publicist to figure out the logistics of doing book tours, countless television interviews, and online publicity while busily writing the follow up to No Lies, a predicted bestseller by all in the industry, my sweet, trusting sister had been living with a monster and I had no clue.

That's when I knew I couldn't publicize my identity to market my book. Paula's safety was paramount and after Billie had to be physically restrained by hospital security while trying to get in to visit 'the love of his life' I knew I had to get her as far away from that prick as I could.

The only person who knows the truth is Chrissie. I had to tell her because the publisher would've freaked over my need for anonymity, and I needed her to sell it. Thankfully, she did —she told Rolf there were safety issues involved and if he wanted the next book delivered, he had to adhere to our stipulation—and I'd whisked Paula away from California to the other side of the country.

We made a fresh start in Atlantic City. It took months but eventually the fear in Paula's eyes faded, she stopped looking over her shoulder, and she trained as a croupier in one of the casinos. I would've preferred her to have a less public job, but I saw her defiance, a desperate need to shake the haunting memories once and for all. That's why she didn't return to teaching high school math, because her joy for anything in the past had leeched out courtesy of that jerk.

Ironic, that when Billie eventually found her almost four years after we'd moved, it was because of me and nothing to do with Paula's job.

Mia snuffles again in her sleep and I watch her, the anxiety that always flares when I think of Paula and what I put her through fading away.

Mia is a welcome surprise, like opening a gift you never knew you wanted until you see it on Christmas morning. I half-expected another bout of rousing sex to quell my need for her. Turns out, not so much, and I want her more than ever. She's like a tantalizing prequel: once you delve into it, you're hooked and become addicted to the entire series.

The ultimate irony? I hate snow almost as much as I hate cats, yet who knew I'd end up hoping for this damn blizzard to last longer than a few days?

With a final longing glance at Mia, I sit at my desk and scan my emails. Nothing from Chrissie but there's one from

Rolf with an ominous DISCOURAGING EARLY REVIEWS in the subject line.

My next release has to do well, because I'm counting on a new contract and a sizeable bump in advance to cover Paula's bill hike at Sunny Pines. It's why I agreed to host this stupid writers' retreat at my home in the first place, because the publicity on social media from the attendees would bump up my profile. Which reminds me, I need to ask Mia if she's posted anything online.

Trepidation makes me squint at the screen as I open Rolf's email and start reading.

Hi Axel,

Spoke to Chrissie yesterday and she mentioned the competition winners didn't make it to your place because of a blizzard? That's bad luck because we could do with a bit of positive publicity.

I'll be frank and let you know the early trade reviews for The Guest Upstairs *have been less than stellar. Readers aren't connecting with the characters and are labelling your plot as trite and 'seen it all before.'*

I know this isn't what you want to hear, but whatever you can do to get some buzz happening online for this book, it can only help.

We're waiting on one more trade review, the most important as far as we're concerned, from the New York Press. Hopefully Mia Samson will give it her stamp of approval and that will negate the rest, but at this stage I'll be honest and say we're not holding out much hope.

Chrissie wants to open new contract talks but for now, we're putting that on hold.

I'll keep you posted.

Best,

Rolf.

Ice flows through my veins as I re-read Rolf's email. Not only does it look unlikely I'll get a new contract, the fate of my upcoming release rests in Mia's hands.

Mia, the woman I've had sex with. The woman I intend to keep having sex with. The woman who will think I'm using her if she finds out her review will make or break my career.

Hell.

Chapter Twenty-Five

MIA

When I wake, Axel has vanished, and I allow myself the luxury of snuggling into the sofa for a few moments and rehashing the memory of what we did a little while ago. The way he touched me, caressed me, pleasured me...Have I always been this sensual or does Axel have some hidden talent for bringing out that side of me?

Whatever it is, I want more.

I go looking for him and check every room in the house, except his bedroom, which means he's holed up in there. I press my ear to the door and hear the faintest clacking of keys, so I back away and head to my room. The last thing he'd welcome if he's in the writing zone is an interruption from a horny woman whose newly awakened libido is making her do crazy things.

Grinning like an idiot, I almost trip over Mr. Darcy sitting out the front of my room, but not even the annoying cat can ruin my mood.

"Hello there," I say, giving him a quick scratch behind the ears. "Just because I let you sleep on my bed doesn't mean I like you."

He purrs in response, and I feel the pleasant vibration beneath my fingers.

"Fine. You can come in for a while, but only because I'm expecting some new ARCs to land and that always puts me in a good mood."

I straighten and Mr. Darcy rubs against my leg for a moment before preceding me into my room. I asked Jace to forward me any new Advanced Reader Copies and I know most of them land on a Wednesday, so I'm hoping to have a few gems waiting for me.

As I open my Kindle, the first ARC that catches my eye makes my heart skip a beat.

The Guest Upstairs by Axel Low.

Excitement skitters through me as I tap the first page and pause to admire the cover—an ominous figure poised at the top of a staircase, the background shrouded in sinister navy and black, with a vivid yellow font—before skipping the copyright and contents pages, stopping to read the dedication.

For A. As always. Love you more than words can ever say.

The bottom of my stomach falls away. Who the hell is A? Surely it's not Adele?

In that moment, I'm swamped by doubt. Was I too quick to buy into his excuse that Adele means nothing to him, and they're not romantically involved? Because a dedication like this implies an undying love and I know there's more to his story with the author than he's let on.

I'm not entirely stupid though and I've already overreacted once. That A could refer to anybody. I've known him for a few days and I'm certainly not privy to his life. He could be referring to a long-lost aunt or cousin or anyone. But what are the odds, when he's already admitted to a connection with

Adele Lavash and said he had no other family apart from his sister?

I'm many things, an idiot isn't one of them. Then again, maybe I am, for buying into his tale that he hasn't had sex in five years?

Has he been playing me all along?

Frustrated by the doubts pinging through my head, I tap the Kindle to flip the pages, eager to get started and immerse myself in the story, a guaranteed distraction.

But after the first few chapters, I'm confused. This isn't the usual Axel Low page-turner. Where's the stellar characterization? The subtle layering of sinister beneath the mundane of everyday life? The ominous hints of evil threaded throughout? The cleverly planted red herrings designed to misguide? The smart dialogue?

Maybe it's my mood after seeing the dedication that's soured my objectiveness, so I continue to read, but by the end of the fifteenth chapter I'm disappointed and close my Kindle cover with a resounding snap.

For a confirmed Axel Low fan, this is his worst book by far.

I'm reeling and an impending sense of doom settles over me when I realize I have an awful choice to make: sacrifice my professional integrity and give this book a better review than it deserves because of my involvement with Axel and my newly developed feelings for him, or be honest and trash it, knowing it will sever any kind of relationship with Axel.

Because if he asked me to go easy on Adele's next book, how will he react if I don't extend the same courtesy to him?

Especially when he's told me about his sister. It doesn't take a genius to figure out that if she has an acquired brain injury she'll be living in a special facility, and odds are the steep fees at a place like that is being funded by Axel. And while he probably has millions because of a decade's worth of best-sellers, I'm well aware of the weight my reviews hold and skewing sales of *The Guest Upstairs* may have a carry-on effect for his books to follow.

This isn't good.

I never should've slept with him.

Mr. Darcy hisses in agreement.

"Mind reader," I mutter at the cat, before picking up my Kindle again. Maybe the story improves and I'm being overly critical because I know Axel now? Maybe I'm just tired? Maybe being sexed up is making me go a little loopy?

But I know none of these excuses are true. I pride myself on my objectivity and my critical literary eye is telling me this book won't deliver on the Axel Low page-turning promise.

So how am I going to break the news to Axel without ruining us in the process?

Chapter Twenty-Six

AXEL

I do what I always do when I'm in a mood: reach out to Paula.

Nobody grounds me like my sister. But I'm unable to establish a video connection or call due to the blizzard so I settle for the next best thing. I email. Besides, writing will center me. It always does.

Hi Paula,

I wanted to chat face to face but we're in the middle of a freakish snowstorm and my internet connection is iffy. Hopefully this will make it through once the wi-fi kicks in again. Can you believe it, a blizzard in late fall? I've never seen anything like it. You would love it. Remember that time we spent a long weekend in Vermont, and it snowed the entire three days? I remember because you pack a mean snowball and I sported bruises for a week after our snowball fight.

I'm supposed to be hosting a writing retreat at the moment for six competition winners. I had to read their first three chapters and synopses after my virtual assistant whittled down the entrants, and I was blown away by the standard of entries. But because of the snow, only one entrant is actually here because she arrived earlier than the others. I expected to not like her, but she's cool. I think you'd like her too. She's funny and warm and doesn't take any of my crap. Like you, she calls me out on it. I admire that.

But she won't be here for long. Once the blizzard stops and the snowplows can get to work, she'll be leaving. Usually, I'd be counting down the days until she's out of here, but the craziest thing has happened. I think I'm going to miss her.

Not sure why I'm feeling this out of sorts. Maybe it's a result of being cooped up and I've got cabin fever? Whatever the reason, Mia will be gone soon, and my life will revert to normal. That's her name. Mia. It's pretty, like her.

I know you'll tease me incessantly for saying that but it's okay. I deserve it, for all those times I teased you growing up: for the buzz cut at twelve after a bad lice infestation, the bangs at fourteen, the pixie cut at sixteen. I was a horror. Don't know how you put up with me.

Anyway, I've got a bunch of fan mail to answer. I still pinch myself that people around the world buy my books, read them, and take the time to reach out to me. The thrill hasn't waned after all these years.

Take care, Sis.

Love you.

A

I hit send and watch the email lag in my outbox for a minute before the intermittent wi-fi kicks in and I hear the whoosh sound indicating the email's gone. I sit back and clasp my hands behind my head. The sad thing is, even when Noni reads my email to Paula, my sister won't be able to comprehend half of it. But every time we chat, I like to include snippets of the past, particularly from our childhood, in the hopes it will spark a nice memory for her.

I lament the loss of my sister's vibrancy every day, but we had years together before the accident that changed her life, and those are the times I try to remember. After I became her sole guardian, she could've rebelled, but she hadn't been too bad for a bratty sixteen-year-old. I didn't go to college so she could, because someone with a brain for figures deserved to do something worthwhile, whereas I'd always been good at building stuff with my hands. Our mid-twenties had been the best: I pulled in a steady wage from carpentry, and she'd been working at a local high school, so we splurged on indulgent things like a week in Barbados and a visit to Hobbiton, the movie set in New Zealand.

I never approved of her boyfriends, and she thought every girl I dated wasn't good enough, but nobody ever came between us and we had an amazing sibling bond. It made it all the harder to stomach when I learned of Billie's abuse. Why hadn't Paula confided in me? Why hadn't she trusted me enough to protect her?

She'd invited me to a survivor's group meeting once and I'd learned about the shame the victims of domestic violence feel, the helplessness, the fear that their abuser will hurt their loved ones. I'd cried myself to sleep after that meeting, because my brave sister had tolerated so much pain because she'd been trying to protect me.

Regret squeezes my chest and I absentmindedly rub it while I reread the email I just sent to Paula. At least writing to her has eased my discomfort at not being able to talk to her. But my relief is short-lived when a ping sounds, alerting me to an incoming email, and I see it's a request to do a podcast.

In an instant I remember the last podcast I gave and the resultant fallout.

The apartment is unusually quiet as I unlock the door and step inside.

"Hey Ant, it's me," I call out, surprised when Paula doesn't

answer. It's eight fifty and her shift ended almost an hour ago, and she always lets me know if she's going to be late. It's a rule I stipulated when she moved in with me, part of my overprotective big brother routine that I'm entitled to considering what happened to her in California.

I quell a frisson of fear and call out again. "Ant, you here?"

It's a nickname I bestowed on her during her first week after moving in with me because every time I put food out, she was all over it like ants at a picnic, and Ant had stuck. It's cute and we're closer than ever. I count myself lucky every day that when that bastard Billie threw her down the stairs, he hadn't killed her.

It's been four years since that awful night and while the fear has receded, it's times like this, when Paula hasn't checked in, that I can't help but worry.

I slide my cell out of my pocket, about to call her, when a familiar eighties tune she inputted as uniquely hers in my contacts starts playing. I answer, tamping down on my first instinct to yell 'where the hell are you?'

Instead, I say, "Hey—"

"Ax, listen to me. I'm headed out of town. Sue from work is with me, because I was giving her a lift home, when I spotted Billie—"

"What the—"

"He's tailing us but I didn't want to lead him home, so I'm going to drive to Pleasantville and pull into the police station."

Dread makes my heart pound, but I need to keep calm. Paula's putting on a brave front, but I can hear how spooked she is by the slightest quiver in her voice. "How did he find you?"

She hesitates and I hear a murmured voice in the background, "Tell him."

"He slipped one of the hostesses a message, said to give it to me at the end of my shift. The thing is, Sue and I were in the car

when Candy remembered, and by then I knew I couldn't lead him home."

"What do you mean?"

"The note said he's been searching for us all this time. That he'd heard you on a podcast about taking a gamble and playing to win, so he searched every casino in Vegas before moving on to Atlantic City looking for us."

My blood chills, turning to ice in my veins.

This is my fault.

My sister is in danger again from a madman because of me.

I pick up the nearest object, some stupid cat figurine Paula bought at a flea market and fling it against the wall.

I expect Paula to chastise me, but she's gone silent.

"Ant? What's going on?"

"He's closing in on us," she murmurs, and I hear the car engine rev as she floors it.

"Don't stop, Ant. Whatever you do, don't stop—"

"He's going to hit us..." Paula trails off, before I hear a blood-curdling scream a second before a screech of tires followed by a devastating crunch of metal, and the line goes dead.

A knock at the door wrenches me out of the past and I blink several times, unsurprised to find my cheeks wet. I swipe away the tears with my fingertips and drag in several deep breaths to compose myself.

So much for emailing Paula calming me. Rehashing the memory of that awful night has left me shaken and I don't want Mia to see me like this.

The knock comes again, louder this time. "Axel? We need to talk."

I can't ignore her. She doesn't deserve that, especially when the last time we spoke it was whispering naughty things to each other, so I shake myself out like a prizefighter about to enter the ring and open the door.

"Hey. What's up?"

Her stare is incredulous. "You're back to feigning indiffer-ence again?" She jabs me in the chest with a finger. "What is it with you retreating to your cave every time we have sex?"

I'm not in the mood for this. But she's right. I have retreated, even if it's got nothing to do with her.

Technically, that's not true, as I wouldn't be feeling this out of sorts if it wasn't for the surprising connection we share and trying to escape by contacting Paula has only served to dredge up a past I do everything I can daily to forget.

Maybe she's spooked by our connection too because it looks like she's spoiling for a fight, so I backpedal. "I've been working, Mia. I have deadlines. It's got nothing to do with you."

A strange expression I can't fathom flits across her face. "Actually, your work is what I want to talk to you about."

She can't meet my eyes, and in an instant, I know.

She's received an ARC of my upcoming book.

And she doesn't like it.

With Rolf's not so subtle warning that my next contract depends on Mia's review, I'm screwed.

Chapter Twenty-Seven

MIA

I don't want to have this conversation.

It will gut me, seeing the disappointment on Axel's face when I give him forewarning that my review for his upcoming novel won't be good.

I've never done this for any other author, give them a heads up, and I'm probably treading a fine line professionally, but Axel isn't just any author anymore.

I've caught feelings.

I know, I know, incongruous and crazy in such a short period of time but taking the sex out of the equation there's something about him that calls to me on a deeper level.

Maybe it's the passion for writing we have in common, maybe it's the way he's revealed parts of himself when he's a self-confessed recluse, maybe it's the way he looks at me, like I'm a wonderful surprise, but whatever the reason, I don't want to hurt him, and that's exactly what will happen if he reads my review before I tell him to his face what I think of his book.

The thing is, it looks like he's been crying. I didn't notice it at first because I'd been too busy accusing him of avoiding me, but now that I look closer, his eyes are red and a little puffy.

"Are you okay?"

"Been better." His tone is abrupt, but he can't hide the devastation in his eyes.

That's another thing I like about him: his honesty. I want to ask if there's a problem with his sister, but for him to look so pained it must be bad and I don't want to probe an open wound. I settle for flippant instead.

"Problems with your WIP?"

"My work in progress is the least of my worries," he mutters, leaning against the doorjamb. "Did you want something?"

I want you hovers on the tip of my tongue but getting physical before I tell him my thoughts on his book isn't going to help. I've used deflection in the past, usually when avoiding unpleasantness involving my mother, and it doesn't solve anything.

"Yeah, I want to talk to you."

"It's about *The Guest Upstairs*, isn't it?" His voice is strained as he rubs the back of his neck.

"How did you know?"

"Inkling." He opens his bedroom door wider as if he's about to invite me in, and my gaze is immediately drawn to his bed and the memory of what we've done there makes my cheeks flush.

His mind must travel a similar trajectory because he steps out and closes the door behind him. "You hungry? I can heat up some casserole."

Food is the furthest thing from my mind and while I can't remember the last time I ate, the thought of telling

Axel what I think of his book has acted as an appetite suppressant.

"Can we talk first?"

"Sure. Let's go to the living room."

His shoulders slump, the air of dejection looming over him like a dark cloud making me second guess the wisdom of what I'm about to say. But it's going to be so much worse if I don't say anything and after what we've shared these last few days, I don't want him hating me when I leave. The snow is predicted to ease up tomorrow, meaning this could be our last night alone together. I want to make it count.

When we reach the living room, he sits on a floor cushion in front of the fire, so I do the same. The room is dark, the only illumination coming from the flames, and if he wasn't so morose, I'd think this is the perfect scenario for seduction.

The sadness clinging to him must be about more than my thoughts on his book and I try one last time to get him to talk.

"I've signed an NDA remember, so whatever you say to me goes no further if you want to chat?"

He looks at me and the flickering flames illuminate the indecision warring with hope on his face, like he wants to trust me but isn't sure. "We've moved past the author-mentee relationship, don't you think?"

I nod, relieved he's no longer seeing me as a competition winner, but curious as to how he does see me. "I'd like to think we're friends."

"With benefits," he adds, with the lopsided smile I've grown to like way too much.

"Another trope," I say, and he chuckles, the deep timbre warming my heart. "We're really living a romance novel."

"With a healthy dose of erotica thrown in," he deadpans, and I laugh.

This is good. We're swapping banter and the tension accentuating the grooves around his mouth is easing. Not that

I'm trying to lull him into a false sense of security, but my criticism will be easier to accept if he's not so uptight.

"Let me ask you something. What did you hope to get out of your week here?"

I hesitate, wondering how honest I should be, because my primary goal for being here might sound like I'm using him. But if I'm going to be upfront about his book, the least I can do is be honest about my motivations too.

"Apart from the priceless feedback I'd be getting from a bestselling author in a genre I want to publish in, I hoped to get some insider information, contacts, that kind of thing, so it can help me ultimately get my suspense novel traditionally published."

He eyeballs me and I glimpse admiration. "I value bluntness."

"Good, because it sounds like I'm using you for an intro into the industry and that's not entirely true. I'm not afraid of doing the leg work, but I know Christine Foley is one of the best agents in the business and she isn't taking on any new clients unless via referral, so..."

"You want an introduction."

"Yes. But only if you think my work is good enough. I don't want you doing me any favors."

The calculating gleam in his eyes surprises me, until I realize what I've just said. One favor usually deserves another, and I hold my breath, hoping he's not going to say what I think he is.

"I think your story has a lot of potential, and with the right editing, it could definitely be marketable, and that's what Chrissie wants. Commercial fiction that will sell and sell well."

"I sense a but?"

He grimaces. "I'm just going to come out and say this. If I do this for you, I need a favor in return."

My heart sinks. I know what he's going to ask and it's

something I can't do. I won't sacrifice my professional integrity to give a false review.

"What is it?"

"I want you to read the entirety of Adele Lavash's *Do Me Again* and give a fair review that doesn't sink the boots in."

I gape a little, because I thought he was going to ask me to go easy on his upcoming book. Yet again, it's about Adele, and I struggle to clamp down on the insidious jealousy making me want to grab the poker and clunk him over the head with it.

"What if I hate the book? I won't lie if it's crap like the last one."

"I'm not asking you to lie."

"Then what are you asking?"

"To put your biases aside when it comes to romance and give the story a chance to impress you."

"You think I'm biased against romance?" I leap to my feet and stalk a few feet away. I hate that he's judging me when he has no idea of what really makes me tick.

"Aren't you?" He stands and approaches me cautiously. "Because it looks that way to me. You disparage most of the books in the genre in your reviews, and even when you give a decent review it's laced with snark and—"

"Would I be writing a regency romance if I didn't like the genre?" I yell, instantly regretting my outburst because no one knows my secret and I wanted to keep it that way until I'm established as a respected thriller author first.

"You're writing a romance?" He's incredulous, his eyebrows so high his forehead is a mass of wrinkles. "Then why...but..." He shakes his head. "I don't know what to say."

"Then don't say anything. Forget I mentioned it. I only said it because I'm angry with you for judging me and suspense is my first love so that's where I want to focus my endeavors on getting published."

I end on a little huff and the corners of his mouth twitch in amusement.

"Regency romance, huh? Carriages and debutant balls and rakes. Must admit, I didn't pick you to be the type."

My anger flares again, tempered with a healthy dose of indignation. "What type is that?"

"The type to believe in a good old-fashioned happily ever after."

The irony. I don't believe in HEA, at least not in real life. Maybe that's why I want to write about it, because in a fictional world anything is possible, whereas reality only serves to disappoint.

I know where my cynicism springs from. Mom's a serial dater and the pathetic lengths she goes to in order to please a man ensures I'll never do the same. It's how I justify never having a real relationship, my sporadic dating, and this short-term fling with Axel.

Because from my point of view, there's no such thing as happily ever after.

"Have I offended you?" He touches my arm and I grit my teeth against the little zing of electricity.

"No, but we've gone off-topic. I wanted to talk to you about your next book." The faster I get this discussion back on track the better, otherwise I'll be interrogating him yet again about what Adele Lavash means to him and I don't want to do that.

Besides, it's self-explanatory. He'd rather sacrifice his next book than hers and, coupled with that declaration of undying love in the dedication, I'd be an idiot to delve deeper.

That's the thing about asking questions. Sometimes you don't like the answers.

"Let me guess. You've received an ARC, read some of it, and don't like it."

I screw up my nose and nod. "I'm sorry, Axel. You know

I'm a huge fan of your work, and I've read your entire backlist, but *The Guest Upstairs* is missing the mark."

He's silent, so I rush on, "I thought your last book wasn't as good as the rest, but I tempered my review because most authors don't hit it out of the ballpark every time. So with *The Guest Upstairs*, I'm going to finish it, but I wanted you to know my initial thoughts because I didn't want you to read my final review and be blindsided."

He's stony-faced as his eyebrows draw together. "You think the review is going to be that bad?"

I shrug. "Honestly? I don't know because I haven't read the whole thing. But the early chapters are definitely lacking your distinct spark and I'm not invested enough in the characters to care, which I should be."

"Shit," he mutters, and spins away from me to stare at the fire. "I wrote it in a hurry. Twenty days to be precise, because I was working on something else, and I didn't want to miss my deadline. I knew deep down it wasn't my best, but I thought Rolf could help pull it out of the mire."

Rolf Shelville is a legendary editor and a small part of me wonders why an editor of his caliber would let something like *The Guest Upstairs* be published. Unless...

"Are you out of contract?"

"Yes."

I hear horror stories about authors being dropped by their publisher all the time and while this is Axel Low, I can't help but wonder if this is the publisher's way of getting out of renewing Axel's contract. If so, it's brutal. Not that someone with a reputation like Rolf would deliberately tank a book—especially when the publisher would want to earn back every cent of a sizeable advance someone like Axel would command —but publishing a story that's not up to par compared to the rest of the author's is either a mistake or a way out.

"So if I don't give your book a favorable review and your

book sales suffer, your publisher may not renew your contract?"

He sighs and turns back to face me, his expression bleak. "Yes."

"Then why not call in your favor by asking me to give your book a positive review?"

He glances away, but not before I see he's hiding something. "Because I'll bounce back but another DNF will ruin Adele's career and I don't want that happening."

I clear my throat because the words I have to ask are stuck. "She's that important to you?"

He nods and a small piece of my heart splinters. "Her career is, yes."

"Okay then."

I need to get out of here before he reads how much his answer means to me on my open-book face.

But as I take a step, he says, "Mia, don't go."

"I need some time—"

"And I need you."

It's a soft plea filled with heart-breaking sincerity, and I stop, unsure what to do.

Axel crosses the short distance between us to haul me into his arms. I can barely breathe with my face squished against his chest and as he tightens his vice-like grip and buries his face in my hair, I feel a shudder pass through him, like he's suppressing a sob.

I do the only thing possible. I slide my arms around his waist and hug him back.

Chapter Twenty-Eight

AXEL

I should've told Mia the truth.

She gave me the perfect opportunity when she opened up about writing regency romance. She'd trusted me enough with her secret—even if she'd flung it at me in anger to prove a point—why couldn't I trust her?

But too much hinged on Adele maintaining her anonymity and asking Mia for that favor had been big enough. What would she think if I told her the rest?

"You warm enough?"

"What do you think?" She looks up at me from beneath her lashes and my heart gives an unexpected kick. "I'm lying in front of a roaring fire with your hot, naked body spooning me from behind, so yeah, I'm just toasty."

I laugh and tighten my arm around her. "At the risk of sounding like a beta hero, I don't mind being snowed in indefinitely if I get to do this with you all the time."

"Careful. You're showing signs of a cinnamon roll hero for sure."

"Nothing wrong with a guy in touch with his soft inner core."

"There is if I expect him to chop wood and wrestle bears and protect me."

Our laughter mingles and she's not the only one feeling warm. "You prefer alpha heroes?"

"I prefer..." she trails off, and I wonder if I should prompt her to finish that sentence, because if she does, what does it mean for us?

"You prefer?"

"You," she says so softly I cuddle her closer to hear. "Too much?"

"Not at all. Turns out, I prefer you too."

I'm deliberately flippant because I don't like the way I'm feeling. Out of control and out of sorts and out of options.

Because there's nothing surer than Mia bolting as soon as the snowplows can get through and where will that leave me? Pining for something I can never have?

I'm a realist. Nursing my sister back to health after she survived that awful encounter with Billie when he'd shoved her down the stairs had opened my eyes like nothing else. And I've been on guard ever since. Too bad that the only time I dropped my guard and let slip about gambling in my podcast, Billie had pounced, and Paula suffered the consequences again.

For the last five years, I've been doing the best I can. I wallow at times and the never-ending guilt eats at me, but I take each day as it comes. I focus on what matters—making as much money as I can to keep Paula safe in Sunny Pines—and don't expect much more.

But letting Mia into my life has made me face facts: that being alone, deliberately shutting myself off from most people, isn't good. She's made me hope again and the kicker is, I don't think that's good either, because ultimately, I'll be alone when she leaves.

There's a quizzical glint in her eyes, as if she's unsure if I'm being facile or not. "The weather forecast predicts the blizzard will ease tomorrow and accessibility will improve."

"It couldn't last forever," I say, sounding too blasé, and she turns in the circle of my arms to face me.

"You don't sound too cut up about that."

I want to say, "Should I be?" but Mia doesn't deserve the pretense. "Maybe I'm trying to protect my beta core because I'm going to miss you like crazy when you leave?"

She reaches up to touch my cheek. "I'm going to miss you too."

I want to ask so much.

Will we keep in touch?

Will you see me when I visit Chrissie in Manhattan?

Will you consider spending longer here?

But I swallow those questions because I'm afraid to hear the answers, and settle for a sedate, "Is there anything else you want to do here before you leave?"

Her coy smile makes me want to kiss her all over again. "Yeah. I want to make a snow angel, because I've never done it before, and I want to explore Sugar Plain because it reminds me of Stars Hollow."

I groan. "Let me guess. You're a massive *Gilmore Girls* fan?"

"And proud of it." She arches her back, and her breasts brush my chest, making me want to ditch our conversation altogether.

But I have a feeling we won't get too many more opportunities like this if she's leaving soon so I want to make the most of this intimacy, something I've never had with another woman.

"Okay. I'll make you a deal. If we both reach a three-thousand-word goal first thing in the morning, we'll do snow angels after that. And when the road clears, hopefully by the afternoon, I'll take you into town for the grand tour."

"That sounds great." Her eyes sparkle with enthusiasm and I can't help but snuggle in closer so our bodies are flush. "Though I think you have something else in mind first?"

She presses her pelvis to mine, and I moan, a moment before she covers my mouth with hers.

Chapter Twenty-Nine

MIA

I've never written three thousand words so fast in my life. Amazing what a good incentive can do and considering Axel's a faster writer than I am, I'm not surprised to find him in the kitchen making hot cocoa for us when I amble in.

"Finish your words?" I ask, making a beeline for the sexy man stirring a pot on the stove, the delicious aroma of simmering chocolate almost as mouth-watering as him. He's wearing dark denim, an ivory cable knit, and a puffy navy snow vest that accentuates the breadth of his shoulders.

"Was there ever any doubt?" He pecks my lips before picking up the handle of the pot and turning off the stove. "One marshmallow or two?"

"I think it's a two kind of day." I wiggle my eyebrows. "I need to keep my energy up."

"You won't get too tired making snow angels," he says, pouring the steaming cocoa into two mugs and adding the marshmallows.

"I'm referring to later," I murmur, and he sweeps me into his arms and spins me around until I'm dizzy.

"Put me down." I swat ineffectually at his broad shoulders, and he laughs, sliding me slowly to the floor so that our bodies are touching along every exquisite inch. "I see you're determined to play the romance hero today."

"Nothing wrong with a bit of heroine-spinning in the kitchen," he says, cupping my face between his hands. "I intend to make today fun, considering it's our last day together."

Just like that, my good mood evaporates. For once, the weather forecasters got it right and today dawned bright and sunny, all evidence of the blizzard gone. Snowplows have been working since dawn so in all likelihood we'll be making that trip to town later this afternoon. While technically my week isn't up, it feels wrong to stay on when the other contestants won't be arriving at all and it'll look weird to my boss. Being snowed in and unable to leave is one thing; staying on when I can, another.

"I'm all for having fun," I say, missing the heat of his body when he releases me, and accepting the mug he holds out. I raise it. "Here's to being unexpectedly stranded in Sugar Plain."

"I'll drink to that." He touches his mug to mine. "And a special toast to the woman who's been an inspiration."

I fight a blush and lose. "I thought you didn't believe in muses?"

"Who said I was referring to writing?"

My blush intensifies and I hide behind my mug, the first delicious sip making me moan out loud.

"Good?"

"The best."

Our gazes lock and I'm pretty sure neither of us are talking about the hot cocoa.

While I'd like nothing better than to dive into bed with him, I know that with the mood I'm in I'm likely to say something I'll regret, like 'can I stay here forever?'

Having a crush is one thing: having real feelings another. I have no idea when my fan-girling morphed into something more, but it's happened, and I have to live with it. Preferably far from here, where I can rehash my memories in peace and wonder 'what if'.

What if he lived in Manhattan?

What if I spent more time here?

What if we agree to long distance?

Ludicrous scenarios because neither of us are remotely interested in moving and he made it more than clear this is a short-term fling and nothing more. I'm the stupid one who's got caught up in living my very own romance novel, sucked into tropes I have no right believing in.

As if sensing my mood, he picks up my free hand and presses a kiss to the back of it. "It's okay."

"What is?"

"You. Me. Us." He squeezes my hand. "We're going to have a great day and focus on the fun we've had rather than the goodbye. Okay?"

I nod because I can't speak past the lump of sadness lodged in my throat. He's too intuitive, too sweet, too much.

Time to get out of here pronto before I start blubbering all over him.

"Snow angel time?"

He smiles and my heart leaps against my ribcage like it's straining toward him. "Yeah, let's do this."

We take our hot cocoa outside and leave the mugs on the top step leading down to the pristine snow that covers everything. The sky is a cerulean blue, a stunning contrast for the crisp white that hurts my eyes.

"This is breathtaking," I murmur, shielding my eyes as I

take in the picture-perfect scene before me. Towering pines dusted in snow, a wisp of smoke many miles away silhouetted against the sky, the shimmer of an iced pond to the right. It's like I've stepped into a winter wonderland, a snowy fairytale complete with a gorgeous Prince Charming.

"This is pretty," he says, his arm sweeping wide to encompass the vista. "You are breathtaking."

He kisses me to prove it, a slow, sensual assault that leaves me wanting more. His lips command, his tongue teases, as he exerts the perfect amount of pressure to make me sway with desire. I clutch at his vest, powerless to stand on my own when my knees wobble.

When he eases away, he laughs, as if he knows exactly how susceptible I am to him, and I shove him playfully. But he loses his balance and, arms flailing, he falls backward and lands on the snow.

He's so shocked—eyes wide, mouth open—that I burst out laughing.

"Was my kiss that bad?"

"You know exactly how good your kiss was." I point to where he's spread-eagled on the snow. "You're down there because you laughed at me for swooning whenever you touch me."

His eyes crinkle adorably when he smiles. "Do modern heroines still swoon?"

"This one does." I carefully walk down the remaining two steps and look down on him. "Mind if I join you?"

"Please." He pats the snow next to him and I lower myself gingerly, thankful he's loaned me a jacket. My jeans will be soaked through in seconds but I don't care, because when I'm lying next to him on my back, enough space between us that only our fingertips touch, I'm exactly where I want to be.

I flap my arms and move my legs apart then together

repeatedly, savoring the swoosh of the snow, the bite of the chill, and the feel of the sun on my face. "I'm doing it!" I yell, exuberant. "I'm making my very first snow angel."

When Axel doesn't answer, I turn my head to find him staring at me with so much tenderness I want to bawl all over again.

"Mia, I want—"

A loud screech from Mr. Darcy interrupts him and I silently curse that cat's timing.

"Hell, I must've left the door open, and he's got out." Axel leaps to his feet and I do the same, agog at the vision of Mr. Darcy prancing across the snow like a show pony before making a crazy dash for the garage.

"I need to catch him before he hides somewhere and gets frostbite," Axel says, breaking into a jog. "Buzz will kill me if something happens to that damn cat."

I follow him but Axel's long legs outpace me and he's at a full run by the time he reaches the garage, where Mr. Darcy is clawing savagely at the door in a vain attempt to get inside.

Axel slows, approaching the cat cautiously, his voice low as he murmurs, "Hey there, Mr. Darcy. It's too cold out here for an indoor cat. Wouldn't you like to come back inside and have something to eat? Curl up by the fire? Leap onto my desk and annoy the crap out of me as usual?"

Mr. Darcy stops scrabbling and stares at Axel like he's about to leap onto his face and claw his eyes out. But Axel's soothing tone has done the trick and calmed the cat. Axel squats and holds out his hand to Mr. Darcy, palm up, and I watch as the cat takes a tentative step, another, before rubbing his face against Axel's palm.

My breath hitches as Axel gently scoops him up, unzips his jacket a little, and presses Mr. Darcy to his chest, giving the cat the option to snuggle into all that welcoming warmth.

And as Axel rubs his cheek along the top of the cat's head, something hits me in a blinding flash of clarity.

I don't just like this guy.

I love him.

<h1 style="text-align:center">Chapter Thirty</h1>

AXEL

"Don't you ever do that again." I waggle my finger at Mr. Darcy, who's oblivious to my chastisement as he laps at a saucer of milk. "You don't like getting wet, remember? And snow can give you frostbite on your paws and tail. So you better stay indoors, mister, got it?"

With a desultory swish of his tail, Mr. Darcy stalks toward the living room.

"That cat will be the death of me," I mutter, wondering if I should go check on Mia now that I've taken care of Mr. Darcy.

When we got back inside, she'd bolted for her room, citing a burst of creativity she couldn't ignore. However, when I walked past her room earlier after drying off, I couldn't hear the clack of a keyboard.

She'd had a funny look on her face after I rescued the cat and I could've sworn I saw the glimmer of tears in her eyes, so

I gave her space. But now I'm itching to find out if she's okay and as my gaze lands on a loaf of bread on the counter, I have the perfect excuse: I can make her a sandwich.

However, before I can get the butter out of the fridge, my cell rings and I spy Buzz's name on the screen.

When I answer, Buzz says, "Hey buddy. Did you hear the good news? The snowplows should reach your place by mid-afternoon."

"Great."

My response is rote, because having access into town means Mia will want me to give her the grand tour of Sugar Plain—and she'll be leaving. A few days ago, I would've been ecstatic, having my solitude restored. But now...something has shifted, and everything is off kilter.

I'm going to miss her.

"So do you want me to come home or would you prefer it if I stay away?" Buzz snickers.

"What's that supposed to mean?"

"It means, doofus, do you want more privacy with your lady friend?" Buzz tsk-tsks. "If I have to spell it out for you, I should be more worried about you than I already am."

"All good here. Nothing to worry about." Which would've held more weight if my voice didn't come out half-choked.

Buzz groans. "What did you do?"

"Nothing." Everything. I like her too much. I want to spend more time with her. I have no idea how to make that happen. "We've ended up getting along really well."

"And?"

"And I don't want her to leave."

There, I said it, and the roof didn't cave in. I glance upward to check just in case.

"Then ask her to stay."

Buzz makes it sound so logical, but he should know me better by now. Complication is my middle name.

"It's not that easy and you know it."

This time, Buzz's exaggerated groan is so loud I move the cell away from my ear a little. "You still haven't told her the truth about Adele?"

"Not all of it, no."

"Idiot." Before I can respond, Buzz continues, "The fact you want her to stay means you have genuine feelings for her and in the five years I've known you, that's a first. Why would you want to jeopardize something so special?"

For starters, I'm terrified of this strange, out of control emotion that's gripped me, and I have no idea what to do about it. I can barely acknowledge I may have fallen for Mia let alone articulate it. Besides, how crazy does it sound, that a confirmed recluse shut off physically and emotionally falls for a woman in a few days?

I exhale heavily. "Because even if I ask her and she stays, what's that going to achieve? Her life is in Manhattan, mine's here. This thing between us can't ever be more than a fleeting interlude."

"A fleeting interlude," Buzz mimics in a high-pitched voice that sounds nothing like me. "Listen to you, sounding like an extract from a romance novel. Grow some balls, man, and go after what you want."

I want Mia.

But will she want me when she learns the truth?

"And you have to tell her everything before you ask her to stay, otherwise it's not fair on her," Buzz says, a hint of disapproval in his voice. "I don't know her at all, discounting that ride from town to your place, but she seems like a nice girl. So do right by her."

I flip Buzz the finger even if he can't see it. "I'm not a complete heartless bastard."

"Never said you were."

Buzz is stingy with words so the fact he's said so many

speaks volumes. The thing is, I know he's right. I need to tell Mia everything before I ask her to stay longer and convince her to invest in us long-term, however or wherever that may be.

But I don't want to spoil this afternoon. When we'd cuddled in bed last night, she'd been raving about Sugar Plain resembling Stars Hollow and how much she loves *Gilmore Girls*. I don't have it in me to ruin her enjoyment while exploring the town, so I'll wait until afterward. Though I'm a lousy actor and hope she doesn't see straight through me.

"What are you going to do, Ax?"

"I'm going to tell her the truth, obviously."

"Good man."

"I don't need your approval."

"Wow, being in love makes you grumpier than usual."

"Who said anything about love?"

But that's the kicker in all this because I know I wouldn't be contemplating confessing to Mia and trusting her with the truth unless I felt something for her. Something deeper than attraction.

I've never been in love. Wouldn't know what it felt like if the emotion jumped up and bit me on the ass. But this relentless urge to be with her, to see her smile, to make her happy, to talk all night, comes mighty close.

"I'll be home later this afternoon," Buzz says. "Want me to bring anything back?"

"No thanks, all good here, though I won't be here because once the road clears, we're heading into town. Mia's keen to explore."

"I see."

I hear the amusement in Buzz's tone and I roll my eyes. "You don't see anything, my friend. Now quit bugging me. I'll see you when I see you."

"Yep, you poor schmuck, you're definitely in love," Buzz mutters, disconnecting after I mutter a curse.

I can't be in love.
I don't know how.
But what if I am?

Chapter Thirty-One

MIA

After Axel's heroic efforts rescuing Mr. Darcy in the snow and the startling realization I may have fallen for him, I hid in my room. I couldn't risk facing him and blurting my feelings, so I did the one thing guaranteed to take my mind off romance: I finished the ARC of his book.

Thankfully, it improved in the second half, but if a reader is like me—with a never-ending TBR pile and not enough time to get through all those unread books—they'll put the book down and not pick it up again. Sadly, I see a slew of DNFs in Axel's future for this one.

It's a shame because he's better than this. His host of best-sellers proves it. He told me he'd written this in a rush and it shows, but I still don't understand why Rolf Shelville wouldn't have edited it into better shape. Regardless, it's too late now, and once *The Guest Upstairs* releases, I fear the book's sales will reflect that many readers agree with me in labelling it one of Axel's rare failures.

I want to be bluntly honest in my assessment of the story but I can't do that to him—it would break my heart—so I pen a carefully worded review that most seasoned book lovers will appreciate, but the cannier ones will understand it's not a rousing endorsement.

Fans of Axel Low will enjoy the author's clever yet slightly caustic way with words in his latest release, The Guest Upstairs.

With a liberal sprinkling of red herrings throughout, the reader is left wondering whodunit until the very last page, where the great reveal is somewhat surprising if a little unbelievable.

But that's one of Mr. Low's trademarks, his ability to shock the reader when we think the mystery is solved and the loose ends tied up in a neat bow.

This one is a slow burn, but Axel Low fans will appreciate another surprising ending.

I re-read the review three times and screw up my nose at the banality of it before emailing it to the newspaper. It's scheduled to go into print next week and, while I'll be far from here and back home by then, I hope Axel's okay with it.

I know it's not my best review. I've hedged, using trite platitudes, and not touching on what readers are most interested in, the characters. But I don't think Axel would appreciate me labelling them as caricatures, cardboard cut-outs of a protagonist and villain, so I didn't mention them.

The book overall is a disappointment and I'm glad to have the review out of the way so I can enjoy my afternoon in town. Though I'm not a complete idiot. It's going to be tough, hiding my true feelings from him and avoiding any talk of his book, when ideally, I'd like to discuss both.

I've just zipped up my jacket when I hear a faint scratching at the door, and I open it to find Mr. Darcy staring up at me.

"Yes, can I help you?"

He meows, loudly, but doesn't move.

"Don't give me those big eyes. I have no treats for you and you're not staying in my room while I'm not here."

But it's not my room and never will be again, and that fact is like a sucker punch to the gut. I've packed my bag and will take it with me, because there's no point in Axel or Buzz making another trip back to town to drop me off tomorrow or the next day.

This is it, my last day here, and while I've done a good job of ignoring the reality until now, there's no denying the facts.

I'm heading home to Manhattan.

After falling in love.

With a man who lives here.

"This definitely isn't a romance," I mutter and Mr. Darcy meows in agreement, before turning his back on me.

I grab my bag, take a final glance around the room, and shut the door, the tears stinging my eyes a result of a newfound allergy to cats and nothing at all to do with my broken heart.

"I thought this would be a good place to start." Axel points to the snow-covered gazebo in the middle of a grassed square in the center of town. "That way, you can get your bearings and choose where you want to explore first."

"I want to see everything." I spin a slow three-sixty, feeling more like Lorelei Gilmore by the second. The red-brick buildings, the old-fashioned storefronts, the icecream shop, the diner on the corner, it all screams Stars Hollow and I'm a fangirl about to go a little crazy.

"You have a scary gleam in your eyes," Axel says, with a smile. "Should I meet you back here in a few hours?"

I shake my head and grab his hand. "You don't get to escape that easily. Fancy an icecream?"

"In sub-zero temperatures, that's exactly what I feel like."

He rolls his eyes and I laugh at his droll response, his dry sense of humor one of the many things I love about him. I know it's crazy to have fallen for him so quickly, and no way in hell will I ruin my last day with Axel by saying anything, but every moment we spend together today will be bittersweet and I must do my best to put on a good show.

"If an icecream isn't doing it for you, maybe we could share a banana split?"

His wicked grin alerts me to an incoming zinger as he steps in close to murmur in my ear, "You're doing it for me. Maybe we should explore your room at the Sugar Plum Inn?"

"You've been reading one too many Adele Lavash novels," I say, elbowing him away and laughing when he clutches his side in mock horror. "I want to explore this town, remember?" I crook my finger at him and lower my voice. "Plenty of time to explore your body later."

He groans and slides his arm around my waist, pulling me close. "You're killing me."

"And you're being a melodramatic writer. Now come on, I'm hungry."

It's a lie, but if I don't stuff my mouth full of sugary goodness soon, I'll be tempted to blurt exactly how much I'd like to skip the town tour and slip between the sheets with him.

I'm spending the night in town because I need to board the train early tomorrow to catch my midday flight home from Omaha, but I'm not presumptuous enough to assume Axel will stay with me. It might not be good for his reputation if he's seen doing a walk of shame out of my room at the inn early in the morning. Then again, nobody knows his true identity and he told me he doesn't get into town very often, so perhaps he won't care. I'm counting on it.

We hold hands as we stroll toward the icecream shop. I like the warmth his touch infuses me with, the slide of his palm against mine, the security it provides. I've never been a touchy-feely person so it's a surprise how much I want my hands on him.

The shop is empty when we enter, which I'm kind of glad about because I let out an embarrassing squeal of excitement as I catch sight of the red vinyl booths with individual juke-boxes on the tables.

"You are such a child," he says, but his tone is soft with amusement and the look he gives me is pure joy.

I'm glad I can make him happy, for however short our interlude. When I first arrived at this place, he looked way too sad, an inherent somberness beneath his gruff exterior. Considering what he told me about his sister, I'm assuming he misses her and that has something to do with his moodiness, but there has to be more to it. For a guy at the top of his game professionally—discounting the hiccup of his upcoming release—he should be more upbeat.

"This place is amazing." I swing our joined hands, much to the amusement of the teen manning the counter. "I think I need to move here just so I can sit at one of these booths every day."

He casts me a funny look, part-shock, part-wariness, and I chuckle. "Don't worry, I'm joking. I could never live in a small town permanently. I'm a bona fide city girl through and through."

"Phew." He gives his brow an exaggerated sweep with his free hand but there's a small groove denting his brows. "Now, what'll you have?"

I glance at the chalkboard over the cash register and zero in on the sundaes. "That hot chocolate fudge, peanut butter icecream combo sounds amazing. Care to share?"

"Sure. Grab a table while I order."

I reach for my bag, and he stills my hand. "My treat. It's

the least I can do after all the glowing reviews you've given me over the years."

I manage a tight smile, but his throwaway comment has soured my mood. I don't want to think about reviews and his books right now, because I'll be tempted to tell him what I wrote about *The Guest Upstairs* and that has the potential to ruin our afternoon before it's begun.

As I slide into the booth and glance outside, I see something so shocking I sit up so fast my knee clunks under the table, hard, and I swear.

"What's wrong?" Axel asks, his expression worried as I shake my head and point to the window.

"I could've sworn I just saw my best friend Rosie walking with your bestie Cole."

His eyebrows rise as he heads to the window and presses his face against it. "You sure? Because Cole said he's heading back to the house this afternoon."

"I'm more shocked about Rosie." I shake my head; it does little to clear my befuddlement. "She's never left Manhattan. Ever. And what's she doing here?"

"And with Cole," Axel adds, sounding as confused as I feel. He slides his cell out of his pocket. "Want me to call him?"

"No. This, I have to see for myself." I drop a quick peck on his lips. "Be back in a sec."

"Wait. What about your sundae—"

I'm out the door before Axel can finish and when I spot Cole and Rosie by Axel's truck, I call out, "Rosie!"

The woman beside Cole doesn't turn and as I get closer, I see her hair beneath her wool cap is two shades lighter than Rosie's, with artfully applied streaks, and she's a few inches taller.

Embarrassed, my steps slow, but Cole turns at that

moment and catches sight of me. "Hey, Mia. Is Axel with you?"

"Yeah."

The woman turns and, while she bears a striking resemblance to my best friend, she's not Rosie, and I fight the inexplicable urge to bawl. It's silly, because I'll see her soon enough, so it must be the feelings for Axel I'm trying to clamp down bubbling up and making me a hormonal mess.

Sensing I'm about to have an inexplicable meltdown, Cole gestures to the woman at his side. "This is Addie."

Addie.

Surely it's not short for Adele?

And if so, that means this is the woman that owns Axel's heart.

She's pretty, with sharpish features resembling a cute pixie, with a rocking bod and exquisite fashion taste: tight black denim, knee-high ebony boots, crimson cashmere top and a killer ivory wool coat that ends mid-thigh.

I hate her on sight. Though hate's a strong word and I don't really, but if she's the famous Adele that Axel's ga-ga over, there's no contest. We have a winner and it's not me.

I manage a sedate, "Hello," before raising my hand and waving it madly in the direction of the icecream shop. "I need to get back to Axel."

I turn and break into a half-jog, ignoring Cole's "Mia, wait," as I pick up the pace. Bad move, as the boots I'm wearing aren't meant for snow and one of my soles hits an icy patch on the sidewalk and goes out from under me.

Before I land in an ungainly heap with a broken bone or two, Axel is there, catching me, breaking my fall.

My hero.

Who's in love with someone else.

Crap.

Chapter Thirty-Two

AXEL

Mia's in a foul mood. Not even sharing the sublime hot fudge sundae can snap her out of it. And she's not talking. I've tried everything, from lame dad jokes like 'why did the vampire go the library? Because he wanted a good book to sink his teeth into' to asking her to name her top five favorite reads of all time.

Nothing.

She's shoveling icecream and fudge into her mouth like she's ravenous but I know it's so she can't answer me.

I'm at a loss. One minute we'd been in here, all warm and flirty, the next she'd mistaken Cole's friend for her bestie, then run away from them like she had a pack of demons on her tail. Bizarre.

' I hadn't gone near Cole because that would mean introducing me to his lady friend and I wanted to focus on mine after she almost sprawled on the sidewalk. So I'd waved and waited until Mia and I headed back inside before I texted him that I'd see him at home either later today or tomorrow, depending if Mia asks me to spend the night with her.

I'm hoping for the latter.

We can't end our time together with a tour of the town. I want more. I want to ask her to extend her trip. I want to tentatively broach the subject of a long-distance relationship. I want to ascertain if she feels as much for me as I do for her.

And to do that, I have to tell her the truth.

All of it.

I'm about to ask if she's finished when she shoves the sundae dish away with her finger and says, "Was that Adele out there? Your Adele?"

"What?"

She pins me with a narrow-eyed glare. "Adele L.A.V.A.S.H." She spells it out like I'm slow. "Was that her?"

Her eyes are flinty and her nostrils flare. She's mad as hell and I'm more confused than ever. Why would she think some random woman who's hanging out with Buzz is Adele Lavash?

"No."

So much for leading into the truth gently. Now she's already fuming and is jumping to outlandish conclusions and will get even angrier when I reveal everything.

She plants her forearms on the table and leans forward, her furious glare implying she'd like to eviscerate me like the cherries topping the sundae that she'd mashed to a pulp. "Then why did you bustle me back in here like you couldn't wait to get me away from her?" She thumps the table so hard the dish jumps. "And Cole introduced her as Addie. Short for Adele?"

I can't help but laugh at the irony of Cole meeting a woman with a name that could be an abbreviation for Adele while he'd been stuck in town. I hate coincidences in my stories, and go out of my way to avoid them, so this one in real life is a doozy.

"What's so funny?"

Her eyes glitter with fury and I'm glad she's put down the fork, so it doesn't find its way to my eye.

I hold up my palms like I have nothing to hide. "I've never met that woman Cole was with. I have no idea who she is. And the only reason I hurried you back in here was because I'd rather spend what little remaining time we have together with you rather than making small talk with a stranger."

The tension pinching her mouth eases a tad, and while her anger has subsided, she hasn't lost the haunted look in her eyes, like she's not quite sure she can trust me.

"I have no idea why I freaked out." She crosses and uncrosses her arms, then clasps her hands together so tight her knuckles pop. "I thought I saw Rosie, and when it wasn't her, I wanted to cry, which makes no sense because I'll be seeing her soon enough. And it's not like Rosie would even be here, so that was a ridiculous conclusion I jumped to." She's babbling and I want to hug her so badly but have a feeling she needs to get all this off her chest. "And then I thought..." she presses her fingertips to her eyelids for a moment before lowering her hands. "I think I'm going crazy at the thought of leaving."

I will her to add 'you' at the end of that last sentence, but her eyes tell me loud and clear that's what she means. And the thought of her feeling the same way about me that I feel about her makes me blurt, "Then don't leave."

Her eyes widen as she stills, as immobile as a statue. "What do you mean?"

"Stay longer. Don't hurry back to New York. Spend some more time with me."

I sound needy but don't care. She hasn't bolted out of the shop and her eyes are sparkling in a good way.

"You know I can't stay, right?" She glances at me from beneath her lashes, adorably cute. "But that doesn't mean I can't come back for a visit as soon as I can swing it with my boss."

Disappointment makes my fingers curl into my palms under the table. Silly, because I have no right to be. Of course she has to return to her life in the city. She has a job and friends and everything that's not here in this small town in the middle of Nebraska.

She takes my silence for regret and adds, "Maybe I can swing an extra day or two?"

I'm euphoric for all of two seconds, when I remember I've asked her to stay before telling her everything, and that's not fair.

"I would love nothing better than to spend more time with you, but there's something I have to tell you." I rub the back of my neck. It does little to ease the tension making my muscles cramp. "I planned on telling you this before, but we got sidetracked and..."

She's calm, with an air of resignation clinging to her, like she's expecting me to let her down. "Tell me."

I take a deep breath and blow it out. Here goes nothing.

"I wasn't lying when I said I have a connection to Adele Lavash."

She stiffens at the mention of the name, and I wish to hell and back I'd told her the truth sooner.

"My sister's bills at the special accommodation in Connecticut are astronomical. I want Paula to be cared for by the best. And she's well-protected there. They never let anyone in to visit unless they're on a pre-approved list for that patient, and after what she's been through that's important. So when I knew my advances wouldn't cover her medical expenses and I couldn't rely on the vagaries of royalties, I started writing under a pseudonym."

It takes her less than two seconds to figure it out. And she doesn't look impressed.

"*You're* Adele Lavash?" She snaps her fingers. "A.L. Of course. Axel Low. Adele Lavash. But..." She frowns and the lips I can't get enough of pucker in consternation. "Why didn't you tell me earlier rather than letting me make a fool of myself?"

"Because the less people that know the better."

"Are you ashamed of writing erotica?"

"Of course not. I'm proud of every book I've published."

Her glare is frosty, like I'm the lowest form of slime. "So when you asked me to go easy on Adele's next book, you were really asking me to do you a favor? Don't you think that's underhanded?"

Shame makes my cheeks burn and I draw in a deep breath before answering. "I can't afford for *Do Me Again* to tank like the last book because there's a significant hike in Paula's bills impending."

I don't want to tell her more, but I have to because the way she's looking at me implies she won't want to talk to me ever again after this. "And early trade reviews for *The Guest Upstairs* aren't looking good, so it's increasingly likely my contract won't get renewed with Rolf. And that means it's even more imperative my next Adele book sells well."

I want to tell her the rest, but I have a feeling it will ruin whatever small chance I have of spending the remainder of the afternoon with her, let alone the night.

She must pick up on my hesitancy because she reverts to angry again, the emerald flecks glowing in her eyes. "There's more, isn't there? What aren't you telling me?"

This will end us. I know it will.

But it's not fair on her to withhold the truth, not when I'm asking so much of her. Her life is in Manhattan, and I want her to stay longer with me. How will she feel if she agrees, then discovers why I invited her here in the first place?

That's the thing about secrets. They have a way of being

discovered and I won't be responsible for destroying her happiness when she learns the whole truth.

I have to tell her.

"Please understand that when I did this, I was only thinking of the next Adele book and how desperate I was for it to do well—"

"Tell me." Her chilly tone devoid of emotion sends a shiver of foreboding through me.

But I owe her the truth. All of it.

"I invited you here a day earlier than the other contestants because I wanted payback. I'd planned on tearing your partial apart, giving you a taste of your own medicine, before discussing you going easier on *Do Me Again*." My gut twists with regret and self-retribution, but I continue. "I'm not proud of my pettiness. And when I met you and reread your first three chapters again, I couldn't do it, couldn't tear down another writer in that way. I'm sorry."

Her lips compress into a thin line and she's shaking as she stands and jams her wool cap on her head.

"Mia, please, I didn't mean to—"

"But that's the thing, you did mean to do it." She slams both hands on the table so hard I jump, her glare ferocious, her mouth twisted with disgust. "And I don't want to have anything to do with someone like you."

My chest caves in on itself as my heart implodes and I watch her run out of the shop, desperately wanting to chase after her but knowing I've blown this.

Chapter Thirty-Three

MIA

I'm so furious I can't see straight and I almost bowl over a little old lady, who glares at me like the idiot I am. A first class idiot for believing a single word that came out of Axel's mouth during my time here.

I've always prided myself on not being as gullible as my mom. Her endless string of loser boyfriends all had one thing in common—they lied to her—and she never wised up. She'd enter the next relationship as starry-eyed as the last, pinning all her hopes on an elusive love that never materialized, clueless she was being duped until it was too late. Some of them cheated on her, some 'borrowed' money, one even stole a sizeable amount of cash, but Mom blithely believed the next guy and I hated it.

I tried to tell her so many times to guard her heart—and her possessions and finances—but she never did, and I vowed to never be like her.

I guess the joke's on me because here I am, in love with a liar.

I slow my steps as I near the Sugar Plum Inn, angry at Axel on so many levels, but particularly enraged because he's spoiled my appreciation of this town. I'd envisaged having a leisurely stroll around the main square after we'd finished that sundae, then perusing the bookshop, before spending some romantic time back at the inn. Now, I can barely manage a civil nod for the young woman manning the front desk as I bolt for my room.

When I checked in earlier, I'd been instantly charmed by it. The color scheme is a pale pink, like the finest spun cotton candy, but rather than being gaudy it evokes memories of childhood.

Mom wasn't big on treats, but she'd take me to Coney Island every summer and I reveled in the warm breeze on my face while stuffing myself with hot dogs and cotton candy. That one day a year when I had my mother's full attention had been incredible and I wished it would never end. Sadly, we'd be back in Brooklyn all too soon and I'd be left to my own devices while Mom went on yet another date. She justified her frequent absences in the evening by saying she worked hard all day—as a waitress at an upmarket French restaurant—so needed to unwind at night. The irony was, she told her bosses she was a single mother who couldn't work evenings because she had nobody else to look after me, yet she was never around at night anyway.

Now, even the familiarity of the pink doesn't comfort me, and I close the door, dump my bag on the bed, and cross to the window. It's huge, with ornate ivory shutters, and I open them further to look outside. I'm on the first floor so haven't got a great view of the town, but I see enough. Like Axel getting into his pickup truck and leaving.

Good. I don't want to spend the rest of the afternoon in

here filled with self-pity and the last thing I want is to bump into him while walking around town. But it's bad too because his departure indicates exactly how much I mean to him.

Absolutely nothing.

Not that I wanted him to chase after me, but it would've been nice to have some indication I meant more to him than... what? A means to an end—to get a good review for his precious upcoming releases?

If so, he played me, just like Mom's boyfriends played her, and I'm not sure what's worse: me being duped so badly when I'm usually savvy when it comes to dating and relationships, or Axel expecting me to give him a good review because he happened to be exceptional in bed.

I press my fingertips to my eyes to blot out the instant memories of how combustible the two of us had been together. It doesn't work and I lower my hands and spin away from the window. Staying in here and wallowing won't help. But I don't want to risk running into Cole either and answering questions about why I'm not with Axel, so I do what I do whenever I'm feeling low.

I open a book.

It's the next ARC lined up on my Kindle, an adult paranormal fantasy that would usually sweep me away with the incredible world-building. But my heart's not in it and when I find myself reading the same paragraph four times, I close my Kindle, open my favorite hardcover notebook—the one with sparkly bookmarks on the cover—and start jotting down words that sum up the story so far. It's a method I've used for as long as I can remember, a surefire way to recall highlights of the story when it comes to writing the review. *Immersive. Dark. Compulsive.* It's enough to jolt me later and I'm about to close the notebook when it slips from my hand and lands face down on the carpet.

When I pick it up, I cast a cursory glance at the page, to

discover it's the one for *Do Me Again*. I listed a few words that night after I started it in the library at Axel's, and a few later when I'd read to the midpoint of the story.

Character goals. Steamy yet sweet. Hero with heart. Swoon-worthy reunion romance.

It's in stark contrast to my DNF for Adele's last book and it makes me wonder if there was something going on in Axel's life when he wrote the last one. I've been to enough book launches and listened to enough author podcasts to know that no matter how many books you write, no two are alike. Even the most experienced authors who've been writing for decades in the one genre admit this. So maybe Axel had been on tight deadline when he had to deliver the erotica to whichever free-lance editor he uses for his Adele work?

I've only skimmed Adele Lavash's novels and spent the most time reading the last, the one I didn't finish, and a small part of me feels guilty I shredded it in my review. Then again, I pride myself on my objectivity, so would I be feeling the slightest hint of remorse if I hadn't fallen for Axel?

I can't believe he used me that way, asking for a favorable review for Adele, implying their connection was that impor-tant to him, knowing it would benefit him all along. And despite his rationale—I can't fault him for wanting to provide the best care for his sister—the way he went about it...he's an underhanded sneak.

As for the rest, I'm riddled with insecurity now thanks to him. I doubt he chose my partial as a contest winner on merit, he picked me because he wanted to confront me and exact his revenge.

Does he have any idea how worthless that makes me feel?

Is my writing even good enough?

I hate that he's instilled this unworthiness in me and that I'll never know the truth, if he honestly thinks I have what it takes to be published.

Because whatever happens, I don't want to see Axel Low ever again.

<h1 style="text-align:center">Chapter Thirty-Four</h1>

AXEL

I hate to admit I used to be a bit of a daredevil behind the wheel, but since Paula's accident I'm a cautious driver. Not that I accept Buzz labelling me an 'old man' when I drive but I don't want anything to happen to me because where would that leave Paula?

Sure, my royalties and everything I own—including the house—will pay her bills for a while, and my life insurance policy is sizeable, but the fees at the special accommodation facility will continue to rise over the years and Paula's only early thirties, so will need care for a long time.

Thinking about Paula is good. It distracts me from the monumental screw-up with Mia.

In what universe did I think she would be okay with me keeping my pseudonym a secret, considering she'd wrongly assumed I was involved with Adele?

I had several opportunities to tell her the truth, and I didn't. Instead, I justified keeping it from her with a variety of excuses: she doesn't need to know, it's imperative I keep my pseudonym secret because being outed will muddy my also-boughts at online retailers as thriller readers and erotica readers don't usually cross genre, and the silliest of all, I liked seeing her jealous because it might mean she cares for me as much as I care for her.

It's so stupid when I think about it. Mia's a smart woman who holds my literary future in her hands and I've botched it. Maybe that's a tad melodramatic, because I have a feeling Rolf's not going to renew my contract regardless of what Mia's review says and he's trying to let me down gently. And whatever she says about *Do Me Again*, I'll make sure the next Lavash release is bigger and better. I have to, because Paula's depending on me. Asking Mia for a favorable review...what had I been thinking?

Deep down, I admit I may have taken advantage of our relationship. The closer we grew over the last few days, the more comfortable I felt in asking her for a favor, something I would never contemplate doing if I'd been in my right mind. But that's the problem. I lost my mind ever since Mia crawled under my skin and into my bed, and I've been making dumb-ass decisions ever since.

I pull into the garage at home, kill the engine, and head inside. I barely toe my boots off and shrug out of my jacket before Mr. Darcy is at my feet, his plaintive meows indicating he's missing Mia as much as I am already.

"Stop that," I mutter, but I scoop him up and snuggle into him a little. The cat's soft fur tickles my cheek and I stifle a sneeze so I don't startle him. "She's been here for a few days. How can you be so smitten, huh?"

Mr. Darcy purrs in response, as if he knows I'm asking myself the same question, and I barely carry him into the kitchen and set him on the floor when I hear Buzz's pick-up pull up.

"Your owner's going to be glad to see you," I say, giving him a last scratch behind the ears before running my hand along his back to his tail.

Mr. Darcy gives another purr of appreciation, which is how Buzz finds us when he enters the kitchen.

"Well, well, well. Someone's made a new friend." Buzz crosses his arms and leans against the doorway. "I thought you hated cats?"

"I do." I straighten and wipe my palm on the side of my jeans, like I'm trying to dislodge cat cooties. "He was making an awful racket, so I had to calm him down."

Buzz's eyebrows rise. "He's always quiet. Why is he making a—"

"He's missing Mia," I snap, instantly regretting my outburst when Buzz smirks.

"Looks like he's not the only one. What happened?"

"I need a coffee for this." Hell, I need a gallon of whiskey. "Want one?"

"Sure." Buzz's response is cautious, like he knows I need something stronger than caffeine to deal with the constant ache in my chest since I screwed up with Mia.

He's always been able to read me. Then again, I'm antisocial and he's the only person I've spent much time with the last five years so stands to reason he's attuned to my moods—most of them bad.

"You must've left town not long after me?" I fire up the espresso machine. "Who's Addie?"

"A friend."

Turns out, Buzz is good at demanding to know everything about my private life but isn't so forthcoming about his.

"You've never mentioned her before?"

"That's because we're friends." His glare screams shut the hell up. "I take it things didn't go well with Mia?"

"Considering I'm here and she's in town for the night, doesn't take a genius to figure that out."

He's lost the smirk and looks plain disappointed. "Let me guess. You waited to tell her the truth about Adele rather than being upfront at the start of your afternoon out?"

"Something like that."

It's not like I hadn't wanted to tell her. Hell, I've wanted to tell her for days but I'm a selfish jerk who was enjoying her company far too much to want anything to taint it. Considering her reaction, turns out I was right to wait. How much worse would it have been if she'd hated my guts and we'd been snowed in together?

"And let me guess, she didn't react so well, and you ran home with your tail between your legs."

"What did you expect me to do? Hang around when the lady made it more than clear she never wanted to see me again?"

Buzz shakes his head, his disappointment obvious. "Did it ever occur to you she wouldn't have had such a bad reaction to your news if she didn't care so much?"

That's what I'd like to think, but I mentally rehashed my last confrontation with Mia all the way home, trying to pinpoint the exact moment I lost her, and while revealing my Adele pseudonym did it, there was a moment when I asked her to stay longer that I sensed a withdrawal, a subtle pulling away despite her flippant response she might be able to swing a few extra days.

I wasn't asking for a few extra days. I was asking for longer. And her insouciant response makes me doubt my feelings more than I already am.

"I assume she cares." I give a diffident shrug, like it doesn't matter how she feels, when inside I still haven't recovered from her walking out on me. "We became friends."

Buzz snorts as he points to the espresso machine, the green

light showing the coffee's ready. "More than friends and you know it."

I have no intention of making my mortification complete by discussing how I may have fallen for Mia in a few days. Besides, no good can come of discussing it. I've botched everything.

"It's called a fling, bozo. You should try it sometime and stop sticking your nose in my business."

"Okay, okay." He holds up his hands in surrender as I fill the mugs and hand one to him. "Don't hate me for saying this, but isn't it time you confronted your trust issues? And if you do have one ounce of feeling for that girl, go back to town now and talk to her."

I understand what he's implying but don't want to face it, so I sip my coffee, knowing my silence will drive him nuts and he'll expound his theory. It doesn't take long.

"You live like a hermit, so consumed by guilt it controls you." He jabs a finger in my direction. "I've never seen you remotely interested in a woman let alone fall for one, yet you don't trust her enough to let her in." He rubs his chin, as if contemplating my stupidity. "It's a damn shame."

I hate how close to home Buzz's observations hit so I feign nonchalance. "You think guilt's consuming me or I have trust issues. Which is it?"

"Both," he mutters, adding "smart-ass" under his breath, before continuing. "You don't think it kills me that I had to turn off Sue's life support machine? That I was the only family she had to make that decision? That she wouldn't have been working a second job at that casino if I'd stepped up when she needed me?" He thumps his chest. "I feel it in here every damn day, but I don't let it rule me, like you do. You've got to get past it."

The bereft expression on Buzz's face makes me want to envelop him in a bear hug. "It's different for me. I caused that accident. I was the one who brought that monster back into Paula's life. If I hadn't..."

I've imagined what it would be like to still have my vivacious sister alongside me every day rather than have her struggling over puzzles an eight-year-old can master. Buzz is right. The guilt that I robbed her of a normal life eats at me constantly. And I'm well aware it's tainted my life since, that I can't function like a normal person because I believe I don't deserve to when Paula can't.

But I can't change it, no matter how much I may want to.

Buzz squints at me, his mouth pinched. "Do I blame you for Sue's death?"

I lower my gaze because I can't bear to see the possible judgment in his eyes, and he yells, "Do I?"

"You wouldn't be here if you did," I mutter, remembering a similar conversation years earlier when Buzz reassured me I wasn't at fault in Sue's death and if his feelings on the matter ever changed he'd be out of here.

"Because by your way of thinking, I should." He throws his arms up in surrender. "The guilt you harbor implies you caused the accident, so you killed both girls, yet you tolerate having me in your life. Me, a constant reminder of Sue's death, a death you caused according to your warped way of thinking." His lips press together in a slight grimace. "Can you see how crazy your thought process is?"

My head is aching like it always does when I ponder what happened with Paula and I down the rest of my coffee, needing to escape. "I need to call my sister."

Buzz's sigh is loud. "Will you at least do me the courtesy of thinking about what I've said? You need to move on, man. Set your guilt aside and start living again."

All I can manage is a brief nod as I head for the library, craving solitude. I slam the door, instantly ashamed of my petulance, and sit at my desk. My hand trembles as I video call

Paula, showing exactly how rattled I am by Buzz making me confront my demons.

I cross my arms and rest them on the desk, my nerves somewhat calmed when Paula and Noni appear on the screen.

"Good afternoon, Axel," Noni says, her tone a tad disapproving, and I glance at the time, belatedly realizing it's almost dinner time at the center. "Is everything okay?"

"Of course." I inject false enthusiasm into my voice and force a smile. "Hi, Sis."

I wave and Paula returns the action, her movement slow.

I study her face as I always do, searching for the slightest change that may indicate significant improvement. But she's the same: her skin unlined, her mouth slightly drooping to the left, her hazel eyes flitting from the screen to the wall behind it. I quell a familiar surge of sadness and ask, "How's everything over there?"

Noni touches Paula lightly on the shoulder. "Why don't you show Axel your latest drawing?"

I can't interpret the odd expression on Paula's face, like she's fearful to show me. Every picture she draws is the same, the two of us in a house. It brings me some peace that she remembers we used to live together.

When Paula holds up the drawing, I'm surprised. The house is tiny, in the bottom right-hand corner, and the stick figure representing me is in it alone. The figure representing Paula, always in a sunny yellow dress, is far from the house, in the top left corner, using a skipping rope in a green meadow. The picture is rudimentary, but the message is clear. She's taken a big leap in disassociating herself from me.

I want to cry.

Sensing my distress, Noni folds the picture in half as I struggle to get the urge to sob under control. Paula can't look at me, like she knows I'm upset, and I need to reassure her. The last thing I want is for her to feel responsible for causing me pain. But before I can say anything, I hear a gong in the background and Paula's expression lights up.

"We have a pianist playing before dinner today and Paula's been looking forward to it," Noni says. "Do you mind if I get one of the other aides to take her to the rec room and we can chat for a while?"

"Sure."

My heart starts pounding as it always does when Noni wants to have a private chat with me. It's often innocuous, like Paula needing new clothes, but my mind always leaps to the worst-case scenario.

Paula waves and I press my hand to the screen, my relief genuine when she repeats the action before going off-screen with Noni. My sister is happy and well-cared for and that's all that matters. It makes me realize that obsessing over Mia and reviews and anything else is irrelevant. I need to refocus on what's important—Paula—and forget the rest.

Noni is back in under a minute and thankfully, her expression isn't grave.

"This won't take long, Axel, but thought I should give you a heads up that the last few times you've called, Paula seems a little sad afterward."

My heart sinks. "Do you know why?"

Noni nods, her eyes filled with compassion. "Her speech therapy is coming along well and she's managing to string together more words now." She picks up the drawing. "After your last call, she drew this, pointed to you, and said, 'hold back.' I think she feels like she's holding you back."

Tears burn my eyes as Noni reiterates what Buzz said earlier. If my brain injured sister is intuitive enough to see my guilt and has interpreted that as meaning she's holding me back, I'm gutted.

"You're a devoted brother, Axel. We don't have many relatives who care about our residents as much as you do." She hesitates, her chin dipping. "I read the interview you had with the psychologist here when Paula was first admitted so I know the circumstances behind her accident."

I'm instantly on guard. "Can you do that?"

It's a stupid question because of course all staff have access to their patient's records.

She nods, her expression sympathetic. "It's been five years since the accident and while it's not my place to discuss this, I want to say something on Paula's behalf."

I want to yell that she can't know what my sister's thinking and has no right to put words in her mouth. But this kind woman spends all day every day with Paula, ensuring she lives the best life she can, and nobody knows her better—apart from me.

Noni takes my silence as acquiescence, and says, "Your sister may not be able to articulate clearly or read like she used to, but her cognitive function is still there to a certain extent, and she picks up on cues. You call several times a week but for her, who can't ascertain time, she thinks you call daily, and I think that's why she drew this picture. It's her way of saying she's holding you back and that makes her sad."

Noni presses her fingertips together in a contemplative pose. "Like I said, it's not my place, but maybe for the next few weeks you could cut back on your calls." Her smile is soft and filled with understanding. "Maybe go out and skip through a meadow like your sister?"

Noni's a trained health professional and I can read between the lines. She's telling me to start living and, hot on the heels of Buzz saying the same thing, it breaks me.

The heaviness in my chest makes it difficult to breathe and my voice comes out a croak when I say, "Thanks Noni, for everything. I'll call in a week."

She nods and I quickly disconnect, so I can let the tears fall.

Chapter Thirty-Five

MIA

After reading for several hours until I'm cross-eyed, I go in search of food. The inn provides a basic room-service breakfast but that doesn't extend to dinner, and I know I'll have enough trouble sleeping tonight without trying to do it on an empty stomach too.

The air is icily crisp but not a snowflake in sight as I cross the road, headed for the diner on the opposite corner. Soft lighting from inside spills onto the sidewalk but as I near it, I see the place is empty bar one grizzly old guy at the counter. The name, Hot Stuff, is written in vivid turquoise against a flaming yellow background, and I wonder if it refers to the food or the staff.

Yes, I know I'm pathetic, hoping that I'm about to step into a replica of Luke's Diner and into my very own episode of the *Gilmore Girls*, complete with cute owner.

As I enter, I'm struck by two things: the tantalizing aroma of simmering chili and how much this place resembles Luke's

Diner. Sure, the counter here is painted purple, not blue, and the bar stools are red vinyl not wooden, but the small tables, the mugs in pigeonholes behind the bar, and the scruffily handsome guy exiting the kitchen with his cap turned backward all scream Luke's. It makes me smile for the first time since Axel broke my heart earlier in the afternoon.

"Be with you in a sec," the guy says, placing a ceramic bowl of steaming soup in front of the old man at the counter. "Take a seat wherever."

I'm having a distinct Lorelei Gilmore moment as I choose a table by the window and I glance at the wall behind the counter, somewhat disappointed not to find a 'No Cell Phones' sign hanging there.

I pick up the menu but barely scan it. That chili smells delicious and that's what I'm having. The menu, like the place, is eclectic, with an all-day menu that covers everything from waffles and omelets to burgers and brisket.

The guy lopes toward my table, his easy smile soothing after the afternoon I've had. "Hey, you're new to town. I'm Cody. What can I get you?"

"Mia," I say, pointing at myself like a dork. "And I'll have the chili please."

"Too easy. Anything to drink?"

A bottle of wine to drown my sorrows would be nice, but I say, "I'm in a nostalgic mood so a chocolate milkshake please."

The corners of his mouth kick up in amusement. "Let me guess. You're a *Gilmore Girls* fan."

I smile and nod. "Do you get many fans like me come in here?"

"Out of towners, yeah. But the locals..." he trails off and gestures around. "As you can see, we're not a popular destination in the evenings."

"The weather?"

"That too," he says, with a despondent shake of his head. "I'll be back soon with your order."

Now I'm intrigued. Like any suspense book lover, give me a hint of a mystery and I'm hooked.

The sixties track playing in the background can't drown out the old man's soup slurping as I ponder what Cody meant. I'll ask when he returns but when my food arrives, it's an older woman I assume is his mother who serves me.

"Hope you're hungry," she says, placing a monstrous plate of chili in front of me with a side serve of cornbread. "Cody says you're new to town. Visiting friends?"

Before I can answer, he yells out, "Stop gossiping, sweetheart, and let Mia eat in peace."

Sweetheart?

Definitely not his mom. I'm a sucker for a page-turning age-gap romance so good for them. Unfortunately, I must not mask my surprise quickly enough and the woman chuckles.

"Let me guess. You're just as scandalized by my marriage to a hot young thing as the rest of this town."

Embarrassment flushes my cheeks as Cody joins us and places my milkshake on the table.

"That's why the place is empty," he says. "We're busy enough in the mornings because the coffee crowd can't stay away from my brew, and the lunch trade is okay, but come nightfall, they must think Tina and me might smooch behind the counter or something because they stay away."

I can't believe people can be that narrow-minded. Then again, I've never lived in a small town so who am I to judge?

"How long have you been married?"

"A decade," Cody says, tugging on Tina's ponytail. She wears it high, like a cheerleader, and her blue eyes are bright but ringed by wrinkles. "She was my English teacher, but we didn't get together until my mid-twenties."

I peg Tina for early fifties so while the age gap is significant, I can imagine in a town this size it's the idea of a student and teacher marrying that has them flustered more than their ages.

"Anyway, we'll leave you to your dinner," Cody says, sliding his hand into Tina's and tugging gently.

But it seems like his wife doesn't get to socialize with other women much because she lingers, staring at my face in a way that's a tad disarming.

"You seem familiar," Tina says. "Cody said your name's Mia?"

"Honey, let her eat." Cody tugs on her hand again, but Tina snaps her fingers with the other one.

"You're Mia Samson." Tina lets out an excited squeal as I ponder the likelihood of my byline in the paper being recognized in Nebraska. "I'm a huge bookworm and I read your reviews in the New York Press online religiously."

Cody rolls his eyes. "You're *that* Mia? In that case, I'll be charging you double for your meal because I hold you personally responsible for the debt my darling wife racks up courtesy of her book buying habit."

I laugh. "I'm honored Tina reads my reviews."

"Read them?" Cody rolls his eyes. "I swear she memorizes every word and is at the bookshop the next morning before it opens to grab your recommendations."

I know my reviews hold sway in the book community but it's nice to meet a fan in person. Is this what it'll be like if I ever get my book published? Having readers recognize me and want to chat? It's a dream I aspire to; a dream I've blown considering how things ended between Axel and me. No way in hell he'll refer me to his agent now.

I've done the right thing in ending our relationship. I can't tolerate liars. But I wonder if my inherent mistrust of men has blown the best opportunity I had to get a boost in the competitive publishing industry?

Cody drops a quick kiss on Tina's lips, and I stifle a sigh. These two are beyond cute.

Tina's staring at me in the same way I probably gawped at Axel when we first met. "Do you mind if I sit so we can talk about books while you eat?"

I barely nod before Tina slides onto the seat opposite me and Cody releases her hand, with a reluctant shake of his head.

"First rule of the diner. Leave the customers alone when they want to eat in peace," he says, winking at me. "Mia, it's okay to say no to my pushy wife."

I smile. "It's fine. Book lovers can spot a fellow literary obsessive type a mile away."

Besides, chatting with Tina will keep my mind off Axel and the fact we should've been having dinner together. I managed to block him from my mind while reading this afternoon—reading has always been a brilliant escape for me—but I know it's only temporary. It's difficult to forget about someone when they broke your heart, no matter how unintentionally.

"Do you want anything, sweetheart?" Cody lays a hand on Tina's shoulder and a lump forms in my throat when she rests her cheek against it.

Anyone can see these two are crazy for each other, even after a decade of marriage, and it's a shame the folks of Sugar Plain are so intolerant they boycott this diner.

"I'll have a chocolate milkshake too please." Tina points to mine and Cody snickers. "What are you, eighteen?" He winks at me again. "No offence, Mia. Tourists are allowed to order nostalgic drinks, especially when they're *Gilmore Girls* fans."

"You wish I was eighteen," Tina murmurs, a cheeky glint in her eyes, before she shoos him away. "Now go, so we can talk."

"Bossy, bossy, bossy," Cody mutters under his breath as he lopes back to the kitchen, and I fork chili into my mouth.

It's delicious, rich in cumin and paprika, and I let out an embarrassing groan.

"Good, huh?" Tina grins. "It's my mom's secret recipe."

"It's divine."

"You go ahead and demolish it, honey." Tina glances in the direction of the kitchen. "We don't get a lot of visitors in here, let alone a fellow book lover, so it's a chance for me to sit for a minute and relax."

My mouth is full, so I merely nod, and she waits until I mop up the last of the chili with a chunk of cornbread and pop it into my mouth before speaking again.

"That was amazing." I dab my mouth with a napkin before sitting back and clutching my stomach. "Though it may take me a few hours to be able to walk out of here."

Tina smiles. "I like to see someone appreciate food. But I do want to pick your brains about books. Read any good ARCs lately? Anything I can look forward to?"

"What genres do you like?"

"Women's fiction mostly. The occasional historical. And I love a good thriller."

She hasn't mentioned Axel which means he takes his anonymity to extremes if no-one in the town where he lives knows his identity.

"I'm reading a few ARCs at the moment, but I think you'll have to wait for my reviews."

I sound like a pompous ass but it's a quirk I have, that I never discuss an author's book until the official review releases. As a budding writer, I wouldn't want my work talked about by a trade reviewer too early—I can only hope I get published one day so a trade reviewer even sees my work—so I respect the work of others.

"No inside gossip?" She glances at the counter, where Cody has left her milkshake, and says, "Back in a sec. I bet he's watching football and can't be bothered to bring my shake over."

Rather than sounding annoyed, Tina practically glows when she talks about her husband, and as she retrieves her shake, I take a sip of mine, wondering what it would be like to be so in sync with another person you can forgive them anything.

I tried forgiving my mom for all the times she let me down. For all the times she put her loser boyfriends ahead of me. For all the times she missed important days at school, like the Science Fair when I won first prize for my spinning solar system, when I made the junior varsity basketball team, even my college graduation. The last time I visited her was the day my first review appeared in the newspaper, in the vain hope she'd finally acknowledge I'd done good. Instead, I found the paper in the trash, wrapped around a chunk of moldy cheese that had been in the fridge too long, and that was it. I was done.

Since then, I make the obligatory calls on holidays, but our conversation is strained as always. I want to talk about work and books, she wants to talk about her latest boyfriend. We have nothing in common. It's crazy to miss something I never had—a caring, selfless mother who'll do anything for her child —but I do.

I miss my mom. I miss her animation when telling me about funny customers she served at the restaurant. I miss her accurate impressions of our surly landlord. I miss her wonky chocolate cakes she'd bake on my birthday. She may not have been around much and she may have been preoccupied by a man when she was, but I can't help but cling to the few precious memories that were good.

The wistful part of me wants to reach out and invite her to spend a day at Coney Island with me, to see if it means as much to her as it did to me. But no good can come of resurrecting the past, especially when most of it was bad, so I stick to obligatory phone calls and try to steel my heart against the pain of having an absentee mother.

Tina returns and sits opposite me again, a welcome reprieve from my maudlin thoughts. "So, about that book gossip?"

Oh, I have gossip. Like how one of the most lauded thriller writers in the country pens erotica hot enough to make anyone blush. But I would never divulge industry news, especially in this day when everything's online before it's barely out of my mouth.

Now I understand Axel's obsession with the non-disclosure agreement. I assumed it had been to protect his privacy, but he must've feared one of the contest winners might stumble on his secret pseudonym and that would've been disastrous.

Not that he's ashamed of his Adele Lavash persona—he'd been incensed when I'd suggested it. But there's a vast difference between an author revealing his identity to the world and having someone else do it for him.

"Seeing as you're a thriller fan, I'm sure you can understand when I say, if I tell you, I'll have to kill you."

She laughs so loud the old man at the counter looks our way and thumps his spoon particularly hard against his soup bowl.

"Stop being such a grump, Fred," Tina says, wiggling her fingers in a wave. "Otherwise, no cherry pie for you."

It's a threat that must hold serious weight because Fred grunts and turns back to his soup. He must've ordered seconds while I'd been eating because the slurping starts up again, louder than before.

Tina leans forward. "Poor guy lost his wife a few months ago and comes in here daily for dinner. Doesn't talk much but

I hope just being around Cody and me helps with the loneliness."

I nod, casting a sympathetic glance in Fred's direction, feeling somewhat mean for judging his eating habits.

"Anyway, back to our book chatter. If you can't tell me anything juicy, let me tell you that as an English teacher, I wish more schools would put popular fiction on their reading lists." She crooks her finger at me. "I'm giving you fair warning, I'm about to get on my soapbox, but I swear more kids would read if they didn't have to analyze the classics. Do reviewers have much influence on curriculum?"

I shake my head. "The school librarians pay attention to trade reviews when choosing which books to stock, but as for curriculum? Doubtful. And I get where you're coming from. I was a huge paranormal fantasy fan as a kid and always wished we could read those books in English."

"It's a real shame." Tina crosses her arms and huffs. "Not that I don't enjoy the classics like the next bookworm. But adding a few dystopian and paranormal novels to the mix at school can only fuel budding readers. And my other genius idea is having cats in school libraries. What kid wouldn't want to be around a cat?"

Tina's outlandish idea immediately brings Mr. Darcy to mind, and I hope Axel is looking after him. Which is stupid because he had the cat ruling his home long before I arrived and I have no doubt Mr. Darcy will continue to do so. But I can't dislodge that image of Axel rescuing the cat in the snow and how that's the moment I realized I had real feelings for him.

"Honey, are you okay?" Tina reaches across the table to touch my forearm. "You don't look so good."

"Just thinking about a book I read recently." One that's filled with tropes but sadly, isn't a romance because it doesn't have a happy ending. "Sometimes reviewing can be tough."

"I'm guessing authors don't take too kindly to having their work decimated with a DNF?"

I grimace. "You don't know the half of it."

We laugh and I'm about to thank her for the dinner and chat, when Cody bellows from the kitchen, "Tina, that apple crumble you're baking needs some attention."

Tina rolls her eyes and stands. "Apparently my husband's culinary skills only extend to savory and I must take care of desserts."

"You make a good team."

Tina's expression softens. "Yeah, we do. Now, if you can spread the word to townsfolk so we can actually make a profit, that'll be great."

I don't have the heart to tell her I'll be leaving in the morning, so I nod and smile, trying to ignore the ache in my chest at the thought of farewelling Sugar Plain and its inhabitants—one in particular.

Chapter Thirty-Six

AXEL

As if my day couldn't get any worse, Buzz flings a bunch of mail on the table.

"Picked this lot up while I was in town," he says, and I grunt in response.

While I get copious emails daily from fans, I'm always surprised by the amount of fan mail I receive the old-fashioned way: snail mail via my publisher or agent. Chrissie insists I should answer each and every one because it builds a loyal following but I'm not in the mood to respond to a fan's gushing today.

Buzz notes my sour expression and hesitates before plucking an envelope second from the top and waving it at me. "You probably won't want to read this one, but I think you should."

Confused, I glance at the envelope he's brandishing. "What do you mean?"

He holds it out and I take it, my gaze immediately drawn to the faded ink stamp in the top left-hand corner.

Hester Correctional Facility

A swift, scorching anger makes my fingers clench and the envelope crumples. Whatever that bastard Billie has to say, I don't want to hear it.

Buzz's glance is sympathetic. "Why do you think he's writing to you after all this time?"

"Don't know, don't care," I mutter, but that's a lie. I do care. I care about my sister and if this creep is reaching out to me, he must have a reason. And I hope it's not to try to get to Paula after all this time.

The letter is addressed to my publisher, and while he has no way of finding Paula, it's the fact my career has me in the spotlight—and inadvertently, Paula—that irks the most.

"You going to read it?" Buzz points at the letter, still clutched in my fist.

My immediate response of "no" dies on my lips because I know I won't be able to rest easy until I know what Billie's said.

That's when an insidious thought winds its way through my dread and anger.

Is he getting out on parole?

He'd been sentenced to eight years for vehicular manslaughter and endangering life. I wanted to press charges for the domestic violence he'd perpetrated on Paula before we fled to Atlantic City, but she was in no fit state to testify after the accident, and I wanted the whole sorry mess behind us.

Has his eight-year sentence been commuted to five because of good behavior? The thought alone makes bile rise in my throat and I need to get out of here so Buzz can't see me fall apart.

But before I can take a step, Buzz lays a hand on my shoulder. "Want me to read it for you?"

I'm eternally grateful for my best friend and I almost nod because the thought of reading one word from the guy that decimated my sister's life makes me want to puke, but I have to do this on my own.

I shake my head. "Thanks, bud, but I'll be okay."

Concern creases Buzz's brow but he removes his hand. "If you need me, I'll be right here."

"Okay."

I head for the library, the one place guaranteed to bring me comfort when I need it most. It isn't an ego thing, being surrounded by author copies of my books and the never-ending awe that I created them, but a need for validation those books provide. They prove I've done something with my life, that I can look after Paula in the way she deserves even if I couldn't protect her when she needed me most. They ground me and I need that now more than ever as I slide a letter opener under the top flap of the envelope and make a quick slice.

A slight musty smell tickles my nose as I slide a single page of thin lined paper out of the envelope, noting it's covered in spidery scrawl both sides.

My gut churns with trepidation as I shake out the paper and start to read.

Axel,

I know I'm the last person you want to hear from. And I thought long and hard about reaching out before making the decision to do it.

The last thing I want is to cause you any more pain than I already have. You must hate me, and it's justified. What I did to Paula...it's something I'll have to live with for the rest of my life. I just wish I had a way of reaching out to the family of the other girl in the car, the one who died, so I can tell them how sorry I am. But I can't and I can't change that either. I can't change any of it, no matter how much I wish I could.

I never should have chased after Paula but I'm hoping after you read this, you'll understand why I did.

I'm not trying to make excuses for my appalling behavior, but violence has always been a part of my life. I grew up in an abusive household and I learned from the worst. Like I said, it's no excuse, and I hate that I became the man I vowed never to be like; and Paula paid the price.

You have no reason to believe me, but that night she fell down the stairs after I shoved her, I knew I needed help. I joined a self-help group and started to turn my life around. In working through my past, I realized I had to make amends with Paula, and it seemed fortuitous when I heard you on that podcast and took a gamble you had to be in either Vegas or Atlantic City.

I wasn't stalking Paula, but I wanted to find her to apologize. Saying sorry wouldn't have changed what I put her through, but I figured I owed her that much. Instead, I spooked her by turning up at her workplace, when I thought that would be neutral ground to approach her rather than follow her. I never anticipated she'd run like she did when she got my note, and I never should've followed her. That was yet another reckless, stupid decision, one of many, that I'll always regret.

I didn't deliberately run her off the road. She braked suddenly when a rabbit hopped in front of her car, and I couldn't avoid contact. It was an accident, but ultimately it was my fault. She feared me, and I shouldn't have gone after her. I should've found another way to reach out to apologize, but I didn't, and the damage is irreparable. I take full responsibility for it and if I could go back and do everything differently, I would.

I'm still in therapy in prison and making amends the best way I can. It's a long road but after finding faith I'm confident I'll be a better person when I get out. I'm up for parole soon and I wanted you to know that this is the last contact we'll ever have.

I've done enough damage to your family, and you don't need a reminder of that.

My plan is to join a life group in Utah; a small church near Salt Lake City that welcomes sinners like me. It's a community where I hope to continue my journey toward redemption.

You may not believe anything I've said here but I have nothing to gain by writing to you. I have no right to ask for forgiveness and I wouldn't do that. But I want you to know I'm truly sorry. For everything.

Billie Adams

My entire body is shaking by the time I crumple the letter in my fist and fling it away. I don't want to feel pity for the man that ruined my sister's life. I don't want to know anything about him, but thanks to the letter, now I do.

I leap to my feet and start pacing, kicking the screwed-up letter like a soccer ball. After a while, the action becomes soothing, and I stop, pick up the letter, and smooth it out. I read it again, slower, and this time my anger is tempered with relief.

Even when Billie gets out, I have the resources to hire someone to keep an eye on him in Salt Lake City or wherever. I don't have to live in constant fear he'll find Paula. She's well protected in Sunny Pines with their stringent security and visitor policy.

So why am I still hiding?

If I finally reveal my identity and start doing promotion for my books, Billie's not going to get to Paula through me. I'm not afraid of him confronting me at a book signing. I can more than handle him. What's the worst that can happen?

It's hard to acknowledge the truth; that Paula's been safe from Billie for years, yet I've maintained my reclusive life.

I haven't been protecting her.

I've been protecting myself.

From judgement. From inadequacy. From fear of failure.

I'm in hiding because deep down I still feel like I'm not good enough and that Chrissie or Rolf or the entire reading community will realize I'm a fraud and rip away the only thing that ever makes me feel safe: my writing.

Protecting Paula had been paramount when we'd first moved to Atlantic City all those years ago but for the last five years, I've been using my sister as an excuse and that doesn't sit well with me.

And Billie's letter, hot on the heels of my conversations with Noni and Buzz, confirms what I already know.

I need to start living my life.

The realization intensifies the headache that is building behind my eyes, and I press a thumb between my brows to stave it off. It does little and when I lower it, Mr. Darcy is at my feet.

"How did you get in here?"

He takes my question as permission to leap into my lap, something he's never done. I brace for him to sink his claws into me, but he merely settles, fixing me with a baleful stare like he knows how bad I'm feeling and I should stop the pity-party for one.

"Fancy the comforting company of another furry creature?" Buzz asks from the door, which explains how the cat got in here. He strokes his beard and I bark out a laugh, the first time I've remotely felt like it since Mia left.

I wave him in, and he sits on the sofa near my desk.

"Everything okay after reading that letter?"

I nod. "Surprisingly, yeah."

"Good." He glances at Mr. Darcy. "Cats are intuitive creatures and I think he may need to stay with you for a while."

"I hate cats."

"I can see that." He sends a pointed glance at my lap, where I'm absentmindedly stroking Mr. Darcy.

"Anyway, he'll have to go home with you today because I'm heading to New York tomorrow."

Buzz's eyebrows shoot up, his grin goofy. "Good for you, man, chasing after Mia."

"I'm not."

Confusion clouds Buzz's eyes. "I don't get it."

"Let's just say I'm finally listening to what a few wise people said, including you, and the letter sealed it." I tap the rumpled sheet on my desk. "By the way, he says he wishes he could find Sue's family to apologize, so it seems only right I pass that on."

Buzz's benign expression turns thunderous. "Screw him. That bastard killed my sister."

For the first time in a long time, I don't think 'I killed your sister'. Because as much as it pains me to admit, I can't control everything. I couldn't control Billie going to such lengths to find Paula. I couldn't control her reaction to flee. And I couldn't control the freak car accident I thought Billie caused but now discover was precipitated by a rabbit hopping across the road, a random act that caused so much devastation. Allowing guilt to fester for so long has led me to where I am today: alone, grumpy, with a hate-on for everything and everyone but a select few.

It's time I made a change.

I give Buzz time to process Billie's apology, but his anger doesn't abate. His scowl is ferocious. "So you've forgiven the prick after one lousy letter?"

"I'll never forgive him. But reading it made me realize I've been using him as some weird self-flagellation tool to hide away and I don't have to do that anymore." I pound my chest with a fist. "I'm done with fear. Paula is protected and I need to stop using her as an excuse to shut myself off."

Buzz's rigid posture eases and his gaze is filled with admiration. "I'm proud of you, man. So does that mean you'll start doing book tours and stuff?"

"Maybe. But first I want to discuss my career and where it's at with Chrissie, so that's why I'm heading to the city."

Buzz's gaze turns cunning. "Is that the only reason?"

"We'll see."

It's the best answer I can give, because while I have a vague plan of how to approach Mia and try to salvage something of our relationship, the execution is going to be problematic.

Because I have no clue what I'm doing when it comes to matters of the heart.

Chapter Thirty-Seven

MIA

"Asshat. Dumbass. Asshole." Rosie counts down her insulting names for Axel on one hand while I manage a wan smile. "And that's just for starters. How about—"

"Enough, Rosie Posey. Calling him nasty names isn't helping."

"It's helping me." Rosie holds up her almost empty wine glass. "Cheers to an asshole-free-zone for the rest of the year."

As I catch sight of Jace entering the bar over Rosie's shoulder, I stifle a groan. "In that case, why did you invite him?"

Rosie glances over her shoulder and I'm dismayed by how her face lights up at the sight of my playboy colleague. Not that playboy is a term used this decade or the last, but I've read enough romance novels to know the term suits Jace perfectly. Along with rakish, devilish, charmer, and cad. My regency romance vernacular is alive and well.

"Jace isn't an asshole." Rosie winks. "He's a plaything."

My eyebrows rise. "A what?"

"Short term fun." Rosie pokes me in the arm. "You should try it."

I did. And the fallout is why I'm here on a work night, trying to drown my sorrows when I rarely drink. Then again, since I got home yesterday, I've tried rearranging my bookshelves from genre grouping to color coding, watching romcom marathons, devouring tubs of choc chip icecream, and streaming reruns of the *Gilmore Girls*.

Unfortunately, the latter only reminded me of the diner in Sugar Plain, and that in turn reminded me of everything else associated with that town; particularly, one grouchy, duplicitous author. Going out tonight is a last-ditch effort to forget Axel before I completely lose it and try a radical haircut, book a trip to Capri, or both.

Rosie taps her bottom lip, pretending to think. "Though as I recall, you had some short-term fun in that backwater town, and I'm still waiting to hear the details."

I point to my lank, unwashed hair pulled back in a ponytail, the shadows under my eyes that are visible despite concealer, and my go-to breakup outfit of skinny jeans, black tank top and grey jacket. "Does this look like I had fun?"

"I think you're pining." Rosie leans forward to murmur, "Jace is almost here so I'll stop talking about this if you like, but might be good to get a male perspective?"

I shake my head vigorously as the man in question arrives. That's all I need, for my private hell to be bandied around the office.

"How are the two most beautiful ladies in the world this fine evening?" Jace drapes an arm across Rosie's shoulders and places a lingering kiss on her lips that makes me squirm.

Rosie merely giggles while I say, "Laying it on a bit thick, aren't you?"

"Ouch. Someone's grumpy." His exaggerated whisper is loud enough to be heard above the muted jazz filtering through the speakers strategically placed in every corner of the bar.

"Leave her alone," Rosie says, elbowing him, and I take some satisfaction in Jace's surprised expression. Rosie may be diminutive, but she packs a powerful punch.

Jace appears suitably chastised. "Sorry, Me-Me. The writing retreat didn't go well?"

The writing part went splendidly. The part where I stupidly fell in love? Not so much.

I summon every ounce of nonchalance I can muster. "It was fine. I got some really good feedback on my manuscript."

And a lot more in the romance stakes than I bargained for.

"That's great." Jace crooks a finger. "Tell us, what's the mysterious Axel Low like? His books are the bomb, and it sucks that fans like me know nothing about him."

If I had to honestly describe Axel, I'd use superlatives like complex, enigmatic, mysterious, gorgeous, warm-hearted. A man of contrasts. A man who can give you the brush-off one moment and rescue a cat he supposedly dislikes the next. A fellow writer and book lover, he's everything I need in a man. And nothing I want courtesy of his lies.

Trust is all-important to me. Mom's antics with her boyfriends rammed that home. I will never let any guy make me feel unworthy and that's exactly what Axel did. I may be able to ultimately forgive him, but I can't forget.

Jace waves his hand in front of my face. "Hey, you spaced out there for a second. Or are you just holding back on us with the lowdown on my favorite author?"

"He's nice. Values his privacy. Gives an excellent critique." And is the most skilled lover I've ever had, but that's on a need-to-know basis.

"That's it?" Jace pins me with a narrow-eyed stare. "That's all I get?"

"Afraid so. Had to sign an NDA, remember?"

"Yeah, but it's me, your other bestie apart from this gorgeous girl." He squeezes Rosie's shoulders and I see the expression on my friend's face.

Tolerance.

So Rosie's telling the truth. Jace is a temporary distraction for her, another guy in a long list of casual dates that don't go anywhere. I'm relieved, because Jace isn't a keeper. He's good for a laugh and his literary insights are brilliant on occasion, but he's not the one for Rosie and I'm glad she knows it.

"So Jace, tell us about that fancy launch party you've been invited to," Rosie says, sending me a surreptitious wink, and I could hug my friend. She's distracting Jace, getting him off the topic of Axel, and giving me time to regroup.

Because talking about Axel has left me oddly breathless, the blooming ache behind my sternum an indication it's going to take me a lot longer to get over him than I hoped.

I sip my soda—alcohol makes me maudlin at the best of times and I don't need to bawl in front of my friends, so I switched to soda after two wines—and watch Rosie and Jace flirt. They are cute together, but I've only seen Rosie in love once and she didn't look like this. When my best friend falls, she falls hard, but we never talk about T.J. And I'm glad. I hate seeing Rosie unhappy and when he'd broken her heart she'd been devastated.

Speaking of broken hearts, I wonder how soon I can escape? I slide my cell out of my pocket to check the time and see I have an email notification. I wouldn't normally check it —I hate the rudeness of people who do this when we're out socializing—but a small part of me keeps hoping I'll hear from Axel, even when I don't want to. Am I a conflicted mess? Absolutely.

I tap on the notification, it opens my inbox, and my heart accelerates like I've ingested a tub of caffeine.

The sender is Christine Foley.

Agent extraordinaire.

I have no idea why the agent of my dreams is contacting me and I'm about to read the email when Jace reaches over and plucks my cell out of my hand.

"Stop being antisocial and talk to us." He waves my cell overhead and I contemplate kneeing him in the balls so I can retrieve it.

A slow-burning anger starts at my toes and works its way upward and Rosie must see I'm on the verge of losing it.

"Jace, give it back to her. She has an early meeting tomorrow and wants to get going."

He appears puzzled that anyone would want to leave a drinks catch up with friends so early. "But I only just got here."

"And the world doesn't revolve around you." Rosie forcibly lowers his arm and grabs my cell, before handing it back to me. To do so, she leans in close and whispers, "You don't look so good. Go. We'll talk tomorrow."

"Thanks." I pocket my cell and hug her, seeing a bemused Jace over her shoulder. I often wonder if he's really clueless or it's a ruse, a way of keeping women at bay.

I wave at him. "See you at work, Jace." I pause, adding, "And be kind to my friend."

"Always." He blows me a kiss and I roll my eyes, before managing a sedate walk out of the bar when I want to sprint so I can read that email.

The familiarity of a chilly fall night in Manhattan envelops me as I step outside—honking cabs, clacking of high heels against the sidewalk, the buzz of people enjoying late night dinners—and while it feels good to be home, I can't help but remember how different Sugar Plain is. The unseasonable blizzard, the crispness of the air, the small-town vibe. I haven't spent a lot of time in various states around the country but my time in Sugar Plain has opened my eyes to a life outside my own and I like it.

I'm jostled by a group of college girls in scraps of silk posing as tops and miniskirts so short they better be wearing decent underwear as I step to the side and check my cell. The email is short and sweet.

Dear Ms. Samson,

I'm reaching out to you because Axel Low recommended I meet with you. I'm not taking on new clients at this time, unless by direct referral, and while this isn't an offer of representation I'm interested to chat as I know Axel has a keen eye for literary talent.

If you could forward me the partial and synopsis of your manuscript before we meet, that would be great. Send it as an attachment in response to this email.

Once I've read the material, I'll set up a meeting time, most likely in the next few days.

Best,

Christine

I can't breathe and my hand starts shaking so hard I almost drop my cell. I reread the email to make sure my wishful thinking hasn't hallucinated it, before closing my inbox and slipping my cell into my pocket.

I lean against a brownstone wall, needing the support before I crumple to the ground.

Christine Foley wants to read my work.

She wants to meet with me.

She wants to talk.

And if all goes well, I'll be one step closer to achieving my dream, a traditional publishing contract.

I can't believe it.

And I owe it all to Axel.

I slide my hand into my pocket to grab my cell, but when my fingers close around it, I pause. Is he doing this because he genuinely believes in my work or is this some warped way of apologizing?

The thing is, I don't want to know. I want nothing to taint my meeting with Christine and if I call Axel and discover this is a ploy to get back in my good graces, I'll lose it.

So I release my cell and set off for home.

I've got a manuscript to obsess over for the hundredth time before I send the first three chapters and synopsis to Christine. And pray to the literary gods that this is the break I've been hoping for to launch my new career.

Chapter Thirty-Eight

AXEL

I'm equal parts excited and terrified as I enter the upmarket deli where Chrissie likes to hold client meetings over lunch. I like the informality of it because sitting across from her at her desk in her thirtieth story office would've intimidated me more.

Even now, after all these years we've worked together, and all my secrets she hides, I feel like a fraud. Like Chrissie picked me from the slush pile by mistake and catapulted my career so fast that I'm destined to fail. Or her client list will get so full she'll dump me. It's happened to other authors, with agents only holding onto their most lucrative clients.

Crazy, because I have an excellent savings account that proves otherwise, but this latest contract kerfuffle with Rolf has reiterated that I'm only as good as my last book and if the sales don't back it up…I'm a goner.

That's what I want to talk to Chrissie about. A new direction for me. My plans to shake things up. I know she'll be supportive even if she doesn't like it. Where I want to go with my career means a drop in commission for her and I'm bracing for the potential fallout: a brusque 'Goodbye and good luck, Axel.'

I see her at a corner table in the back, perusing the menu. She's still favoring the tortoiseshell-rimmed spectacles she'd been wearing when we met last week at that warehouse café.

Has it only been less than two weeks since Mia whirled into my life and upended it? Feels like a lifetime ago. So much has happened…but I can't think about that now. I need to focus. Chrissie's specs are in danger of falling off her nose and she pushes them up absentmindedly, an action I've seen countless times before. I like that Chrissie appears approachable yet formidable, her friendly demeanor underlined by a steely determination that serves her clients well in negotiations.

She senses my approach and glances up as I reach the table, her smile warm as usual. "Axel. Good to see you."

"Same." I lean down to hug her, before sitting opposite. "Thanks for meeting me."

"Must say, it's a surprise, you making a trip to the city twice in under two weeks." She pins me with an astute stare. "Was being snowed in with Mia Samson that bad?"

"No, but that's what I want to talk to you about, what happened while she was at my place."

"Considering you referred her to me as a potential client, I'm assuming it went well?"

She doesn't know the half of it. Connecting with Mia, letting her into my life and my heart, had been amazing. Pity it had gone downhill from there.

"Mia's got talent and I think her manuscript is sellable, what I've read of it."

Chrissie's eyebrow arches. "That's a rousing endorsement coming from you."

"She deserves it."

Mia deserves a lot more but it's a start; the least I can do for lying to her when I had countless opportunities to tell her the truth.

"But that's not why I'm here." I interlock my fingers under the table and straighten my shoulders. "I want us to have a frank discussion about my next contract," I say, noting the slightest shift of Chrissie's gaze before she refocuses on me. "You don't need to spell it out. Rolf isn't renewing my option, is he?"

Chrissie shakes her head, surprisingly stoic. Then again, authors get dumped by publishers all the time and she's probably used to delivering bad news. "I don't think so. I called him yesterday to put out feelers after he sent that email about the trade reviews for *The Guest Upstairs* being less than stellar, and he was blunt. If sales of the book don't surpass the last book, they're dropping you."

I brace for the panic to set in, that familiar overwhelming feeling of "maybe I'm not good enough" that grips me on release day for every book I've had published. But today, it doesn't come. And I know why. In exploring my options, I know I'm good enough to weather whatever proverbial storm comes my way. I'm not a newbie anymore. I can do this.

"Okay."

Chrissie appears incredulous at my low-key reaction. "You're not mad? Disappointed?"

I shrug. "I'm a realist and by the tone of that email I knew what was coming."

Not surprisingly, there's a determined glint in her eyes. "We can pitch your next idea elsewhere. You've got a good track record."

"But any other publisher will consider the sales of my last book, won't they?"

"Yes, but I can spin anything."

She has reservations. I can tell. She's not quite as upbeat as she usually is at the thought of pitching something new.

"But?"

Chrissie steeples her fingers and rests her forearms on the table. "But you're right, in this industry you're only as good as your last book. And while you've been commanding big advances and selling through, if *The Guest Upstairs* tanks, it's going to be tough."

If she appears disappointed now, wait until she hears my plan.

Here goes nothing.

"I want to move in a different direction. Give the suspense a rest for a while."

I don't have to spell it out, the spark of understanding in her eyes is immediate.

"You want to focus on the erotica?"

I nod, relieved to have it out in the open. "I'm tired of hiding. I need a significant boost in income, and I want to start promoting. All my books, actually, so if Rolf wants me to do a book tour for this upcoming release, I'm all for it."

She gapes for a full five seconds before closing her mouth. "But what about that abusive—"

"He can't hurt Paula, not anymore. And I've realized that I'm using him as an excuse to hide when I don't have to now." I clear my throat, surprised by the swell of emotion. "I want to make changes and it's time my fans met Axel Low and Adele Lavash, don't you think?"

She's beaming. "I won't lie, having you do a tour with book signings in stores, library visits, that kind of thing, will boost your profile and your sales. Would you be amenable to a new contract if Rolf offers one or do you want to focus on the indie stuff?"

I know what she's asking. Chrissie doesn't get commission on my indie work so if I don't accept a contract from a publisher, she won't earn a cent from whatever I publish in the next year or so. But I've made this decision and I want to stick with it.

"I want to focus on indie publishing for a while. Are you okay with that? Because I understand if you'd rather drop me—"

"Axel, stop." She holds up her hand. "I earn a sizeable salary from your backlist royalties, not to mention my fifteen percent on your big advances over the last decade." She smiles with approval. "You're a creative and you need to do what feeds your muse. If this is what you want to do, I'll back you one hundred percent."

"Thanks Chrissie." I reach for a glass of water and take several gulps to ease the tightness in my throat.

"You do know that revealing yourself as the author behind the Adele Lavash pseudonym is going to invite critics to pile on with the usual drivel, like men can't write romance let alone erotica, that you're jumping on a trend trying to make a fast buck, that kind of thing?"

"I can handle it."

If I survived Mia leaving me and taking my heart with her, I can handle anything.

"Okay then. While you order, I'll fire off an email to Rolf and let him know the good news. Then later you can call your publicist and start the ball rolling?"

"Sure. What are you having?"

"The usual."

For as long as she's been representing me and we meet here, Chrissie orders the Reuben, with the deli's homemade pickles rather than sauerkraut. The familiarity comforts me because I know once we finish lunch, a new stage in my writing career is about to begin and my bravado only extends so far.

She thanked me for referring Mia and I want to ask if she's

reached out to her, but it's not my place. Unless…I'm in the city where Mia lives. I want to apologize and tell her everything. What better way to do that than with Chrissie acting as a go-between?

Once I order and pay at the counter, I return to the table to find Chrissie smirking.

"What's that look for?"

"I thought you might like to know your referral is meeting me here after we finish."

My heart does a weird shimmy that makes me breathless. "Mia's coming here?"

Chrissie snaps her fingers. "I knew it." She points at my face. "I had a feeling something happened between you two and by your eager expression, I'm right."

I manage a sheepish grin. "I wanted to talk to you about that. I messed up with Mia and rather than reach out to her direct, I was going to ask you when you were meeting her so I could show up afterward."

Her disapproving frown tells me what she thinks of that idea. "I thought you had more guts than that. If you don't want to call, how about emailing her like a normal person and reaching out yourself?"

If I call she'll screen or hang up on me, and she'll probably ignore my email or formulate some trite response I have no hope of interpreting. If I see her face to face, I'll be able to gauge her reaction to my apology better and figure out if I have a hope in hell of persuading her to forgive me.

"You're right," I say. "But I'm still going to take my chances and wait until you finish meeting with her."

"You're insane." Chrissie shakes her head, but I glimpse amusement in her eyes. "Or in love."

It's too soon to tell if I am but for the first time in my life, I'm open to the possibility.

Chapter Thirty-Nine

MIA

I've never been this nervous as I enter the deli and spot Christine Foley, her nose buried in a book. Reading is part of her job but seeing a fellow book lover so absorbed in a paperback calms me a little. We have that in common, our love of books, and if I can't string two words together when she asks me about my manuscript I can always resort to talking about our favorite novels.

I've researched countless ways to pitch a novel online—focus on where the story is set, highlight the main protagonists, mention the inciting incident, make comparisons to well-known projects—and I'm fairly confident I can answer any questions she may have about my manuscript. But all I can think is *one of the best agents in the business wants to meet with me to discuss the story I wrote and may offer to represent me.*

Whatever the outcome from this meeting, I know I have to contact Axel and thank him. I dithered over sending him a quick email late last night when I was too wound up over this

"

potential meeting to sleep, but considering the connection we shared—despite it imploding at the end—it needs to be done right. If I had his number I'd call him, but I don't: the only contact information the competition winners were given was his email, and I try not to dwell that he has my number from my entry but hasn't used it to apologize or otherwise.

So I'll have to email him but I need a clear head to formulate what I'm going to say. And with a little luck, I'll have exciting news to tell him after this meeting.

Not that I expect Christine to offer to represent me on the spot, but a girl can always live in hope.

I take a few deep breaths, smooth down my jacket, and hoist my bag higher on my shoulder as I approach the table. I mentally rehearse my introduction but can't come up with anything more scintillating than 'hi, I'm Mia Samson.'

The deli is packed with a late lunchtime crowd, and I hope I don't have to shout to be heard when we talk. A pungent aroma of brisket wars with fried onions, and the sudden queasiness in my stomach has nothing to do with the smells emanating from the kitchen and everything to do with my rampant nerves as I reach the table.

Christine glances up, her smile welcoming as she closes the book and slides it into her bag before I can see the cover. She stands and holds out her hand, while I hope mine isn't too sweaty.

"Christine Foley. Pleased to meet you, Mia."

"Likewise." I shake her hand. "Thanks for inviting me to chat with you."

"After reading the synopsis and partial of your manuscript, I had to." She gestures at the seat opposite hers. "Please, have a seat. Would you like something to eat?"

I can barely force words past the tightness in my throat; swallowing food would be impossible. "No thanks."

"Coffee?"

"Water's fine." There's a squat aqua bottle on the table and two glasses, so I sit and fill them to the brim, before gulping half of mine to ease my nerves.

There's an understanding glimmer in her eyes. She's probably used to new authors being awestruck in her presence. "So, first up, let me say I love what I've read so far of Kill Me Now. Is the manuscript complete?"

She loves what she's read. She *loves* it? Elation expands like a balloon in my chest. "A first draft, yes. But it needs a lot of editing."

I don't tell her how many times I edited those first three chapters before sending them to her. She'll think I'm more obsessive than I am, which is a lot.

"Good, because it's easier to sell a complete manuscript, especially if it's your first."

I zero in on one word.

Sell.

Christine Foley thinks she can sell my manuscript?

I grip the underside of the table to prevent from slithering to the floor in an undignified heap. I try to formulate an intelligent question, something that will show I'm a professional, but my mind is blank.

Ever since I started writing a year ago, I've dreamed of this moment. I visualized an agent loving my story enough to represent me and to ultimately sell it. It's the first thing I think of when I open my eyes every morning and last thing at night before I drift off to sleep. I read somewhere that visualizing your goals can manifest them and that's what I've been doing, never in my wildest dreams thinking it will come true.

"Is this the first story you've written?"

"Yes, the first I've completed." I won't tell her about the regency romance just yet. I haven't written more than two chapters, so I want to focus on the manuscript I've completed.

The partial she's read and loved. *Loved.* "I've been wanting to write suspense for ages so thought I'd give it a try."

"You definitely have talent, but as I'm sure you know, making it in this business takes more than that. Is that what you want, to make a career out of writing, or are you merely dabbling while focusing on climbing the editorial ladder at the newspaper?"

I want to answer her as honestly as I can without sounding like a complete dreamer. Then again, she represents writers. She'll be used to this.

"Like many writers, I'm a bookworm. I can read all day and night if given the opportunity. It's why I majored in English Literature at college, why I interned at a publishing house, before being lucky enough to land my dream job of reading books for a living. But somewhere along the line, the dream changed. I want to be traditionally published. I want to walk into a bookstore and hold my book in my hands. I want to earn a living from creating words rather than critiquing others."

She nods in approval. "So this isn't just a passing fad for you?"

"If you're asking if I want to be a one hit wonder, then no. I'm in this for the long haul, willing to write as many books as a publisher who has faith in me wants."

Once again, I've said the right thing because some of the tension lines around her mouth ease. "Advances for debut authors in this genre can be lowball. Are you okay with that?"

The thought of being paid anything by a publisher sends me into a tailspin of giddy excitement, but I manage a sedate nod. "I'll still be working at the paper so yes."

She's staring at me so intently I get the feeling she's sizing me up and I hope she likes what she sees. I've worn my best suit, a charcoal pinstripe jacket and mid-calf skirt ensemble with a red silk top beneath. Classy and powerful is the look

I'm going for. A professional who's ready to take the publishing world by storm.

"It won't be a conflict of interest for you? Reviewing other authors while having your book being reviewed?"

"As long as I don't give myself a glowing five-star review, I don't see a problem."

She laughs at my droll response, and I join in, trying not to cross my fingers under the table. Christine wouldn't be asking all these questions unless she thinks my book has the potential of being bought and I'm struggling to contain my excitement.

"I've always liked your reviews," she says. "They're insightful, concise, and fair. And your natural voice shines through in what I've read of your story." Christine eyeballs me and smiles. "If you're interested, I'd love to represent you."

I let out a little squeal of excitement. So much for professionalism, but I can't help myself, and her smile broadens.

"Is that a yes?"

"Definitely a yes. Thank you so much." I'm reeling, but in my euphoria, I know I have to tell her the truth about my hopes for the future. "Though full disclosure, I'm dabbling with a regency romance at the moment too, and I'm having a ball with it so would like to also head in that direction in the future, but suspense is my first love and I have no idea if I'll finish the regency and—"

"Take a breath," Christine says, with a chuckle. "I'm happy to take a look at it for you, but you'll need to use a pseudonym if you want to pursue the romance path too, otherwise if both books sell and you're trying to establish a brand, there can be confusion for readers."

"I totally understand."

The thought of Christine selling any books for me is mind-blowing, but the prospect of publishing both stories in genres I love, I can barely comprehend it.

"Now, if you don't mind, I have an editorial meeting I

have to attend." She stands and picks up her bag. "I'll email you my agency contract. If you have any questions, don't hesitate to ask." She holds out her hand. "Welcome aboard, Mia."

I shake her head, relieved mine's not trembling. "Thanks, Christine. I'm excited to work with you."

"Likewise."

I can't move for a full thirty seconds after she leaves. My head is whirring with the implications of being represented by a top agent and my body is numb. I must be in shock, but in the best way. My heart is racing, and I want to leap up, run through the deli, and let out an exultant whoop, but I remain seated, staring at the empty chair opposite me, wondering if I imagined the last ten minutes.

I now have an agent.

One of the best.

She loves my manuscript.

She thinks she can sell it.

One crazy thought after another pings through my head and I close my eyes and take calming breaths. I hoped this would happen one day, but to have it expedited courtesy of Axel...I owe him.

I need to email him and hope he'll give me his address so I can send a gift basket. That's the thing about being picked up by Cole at the train station when I first arrived in town and driven into the middle of Sugar Plain countryside. I have no idea of where Axel actually lives.

I'll send the email now, but when I open my eyes, I see the man I want to thank sitting in the chair Christine has vacated, like I've conjured him up out of thin air.

Chapter Forty

AXEL

"Surprise."

It's the lamest greeting ever and I inwardly cringe as Mia gapes at me like I'm a mirage.

"What are you doing here?"

"I had a meeting with Christine here earlier and she mentioned she'd be seeing you after me, so I hung around." I point to a table near the front window. "I've been biding my time in the hope you'll hear me out."

Thankfully, she doesn't look mad. "Actually, I was just thinking about you."

"Good things, I hope."

"This time, yes."

Which means she probably spent every moment after she left Sugar Plain thinking bad things about me. I don't blame her. I gave her every reason not to trust me and I hope to rectify that now.

"What were you thinking?"

She settles back in her chair and her gaze is direct rather than hostile. "That I'd like to send you a book box gift, filled with new hardcovers and bookmarks and candles if I knew your address."

Confused by her wanting to send me a gift when I deserve the opposite, my eyebrows rise, and she smiles. "As a thank you for facilitating an introduction with Christine." Her eyes virtually sparkle, and I know what's coming before she speaks. "She offered to represent me."

Her joyous expression makes my heart swell. "That's great, Mia, I'm really happy for you."

I want to hug her so badly. Instead, I reach across the table with the intent to snag her hand, but she guesses my intention and folds her arms. So I'm not entirely forgiven and her pulling away fills me with disappointment.

"Thanks. I'm ecstatic and can hardly believe it." She pauses and her smile fades. "But what are you doing here?"

"By here do you mean the city?"

She rolls her eyes, and it catapults me back to the first day we met when she did the same. Back then, I'd been determined to dislike her, to prove a stupid point because of my wounded ego. But Mia Samson is all too likeable, and I need to do whatever it takes to get her to forgive me.

Her lips press into a thin line as she glares at me with blatant suspicion. "Why did you want to see me?"

"Because I wanted to apologize for how things ended between us—"

"No explanation necessary." Her interruption is emphatic, and I know I have my work cut out for me. "We had a fling. That's it. What you did and didn't tell me at the time is of no consequence now."

"But it is." She must hear the desperation in my tone because she appears faintly startled, and I temper my voice. "I've spent so long shutting myself off from everybody that when I started to have real feelings for you, I didn't know how to act let alone trust you enough to allow you in."

She's silent, watching me with a quiet intensity, so I continue. "I've always been an introvert. I already told you my folks died within months of each other when I was eighteen and Paula was sixteen. I was so overwhelmed with being the only family she had I started writing down my feelings. It's how I fell in love with writing. But I never thought I could earn a living off it, so I did carpentry. I couldn't go to college because I had to look after Paula, and I was overprotective so naturally she rebelled, going out with the bad boys, and that continued until she met Billie."

Despite Billie sending that letter, thinking about him let alone saying his name still makes bile churn in my gut. "She met him because of me. We were out celebrating my first contract at a bar and that's how they met. She was smitten, me less so, but she moved in with him soon after and I realized I had to let go." My jaw tightens. "I didn't know about the abuse until a year later when she ended up in hospital with broken bones all over her body after he shoved her down the stairs."

I glimpse tears in Mia's eyes and this time, she reaches out to me, and I let her take my hand. "I'm so sorry, Axel."

I hate recounting one of the worst times in my life. Seeing the sister entrusted to my care so broken had gutted me. I should've been more aware. I should've seen something was wrong. I should've been the kind of brother she could confide in. Instead, I'd been clueless until it had been too late and that's something I have to live with.

But wallowing in guilt isn't conducive to having a life with Mia, and that's what I want. And to do that, I need to open up despite every self-preservation mechanism telling me not to.

"It was awful, seeing her like that. I wanted to kill the guy, but she didn't want to press charges. She just wanted to escape." My hands clench into fists at the memory of how badly I'd wanted to inflict the same damage on Billie. The only thing that stopped me was the thought of Paula being alone and unprotected if I went to jail and I couldn't have that, not when I'd already let her down so badly. "When she recovered, we moved across the country."

Understanding sparks her eyes. "That's why you don't do publicity and have no online presence?"

I nod. "I had to keep her safe, so I told Christine everything, and she pushed for the stipulation in my contract that I keep my identity protected. Axel is my first name, but Low is a pseudonym. My surname is Moore."

Even saying it out loud feels like a big step and thankfully, Mia squeezes my hand in silent encouragement.

"We moved far from California to Atlantic City, she lived with me, and I did everything I could to be there for her. My career took off and Paula, who'd been teaching high school math in LA, got a job as a croupier because she wanted a complete break from the past. We were doing okay after a few years..."

Better than okay. As more time passed, I watched my sister heal before my eyes. Not physically, because her bones mended back in LA, but mentally, she started to trust her instincts again. She attended a local art studio and indulged a long-hidden passion for pottery. She learned to cook Thai food and loved accompanying me to shop for groceries every week. When she got promoted at the casino, her confident glow returned. She even dated a few guys, but not before I vetted them thoroughly. She'd hated that, but she'd understood.

After the car accident, I wondered if our sedate lives had lulled me into a false sense of security. Would I have done that interview if Paula hadn't been doing so well and I'd been over-confident in my ability to protect her? Sadly, I'll never know.

"Unfortunately, because I thought we were doing okay, I got sloppy. A prominent interviewer reached out to me, and I agreed to be a guest on his podcast. But I slipped up and mentioned something about gambling during the interview, so when the podcast went viral, Billie figured out we must be in a casino city and the two obvious choices were Vegas or Atlantic City. He discovered where Paula worked and followed her..." I shake my head against the futility of it all. "She panicked with him chasing her and crashed the car. That's how she got the acquired brain injury and how Sue, Cole's sister who worked with her, died."

"Oh my..." Mia blinks rapidly to stave off tears, but one escapes and trickles down her cheek.

I wipe it away with my thumb, squeezing her other hand with mine.

"That's how Cole and I met. He had to turn off Sue's life support. We were two loners floundering. I thought he'd hate my guts and hold Paula and me responsible, but we bonded, I offered him a place to stay, and we've been best buddies ever since."

To her credit, she senses I'm on a roll and doesn't interrupt me. I'm glad, because if I don't get this all out in one go my courage might desert me.

"I want Paula to have the best care and her bills are expensive, so that's why I started writing erotica. I jumped on a trend, and it took off. Did I churn books out quickly and were they edited less than my thrillers? Yes. Did I care? No, because it's all about the money. So when you threatened that with your DNF and my sales plummeted, I went a little loopy." I make circles at my temple. "I've already apologized for my intent to wreak revenge by tearing apart your work, but it's still appalling, I know."

Revealing the rest will make or break us and I inhale a deep breath, blow it out, trying to settle my rampant nerves.

"For the last five years, I've been a recluse. I've wallowed in my guilt, allowing it to taint everything. I've grown so used to blaming myself for Paula's predicament the only thing that provides solace is my writing. It's like therapy for me, and I didn't want anyone to mess with that, particularly a snarky reviewer."

Her eyes widen but I need to say the rest. "I don't trust easily, and I don't let anyone in. Until you. You bowled into my house and wouldn't back down no matter how grumpy I was. You called my bluff. You intrigued me and captivated me, and I might have fallen in love with you."

Drained, I slump in my chair and sadly, when I try to remove my hand from hers, she lets me.

She doesn't say anything and my heart thumps so loudly I can feel it reverberating through my body. I can't get a read on her. She's not moving. Her expression is blank.

I've blown it.

Then I glimpse the barest twitch at the corner of her mouth, like she wants to smile, and hope warms me.

"That's some speech. Did you write that down and practice it before coming here today?"

"No. That's from the heart."

"So you don't write from the heart usually?"

She's twisting my words, like she's addled my brain from the start. "I write fiction. You and me and what we feel for each other? It's fact."

At least, I'm hoping it is, because I've just told her I love her, and she hasn't returned the sentiment.

"I have major trust issues too. I grew up with my mom having a string of loser boyfriends who broke her heart over and over. I date sporadically because of it. Then I met you." She jabs a finger in my direction. "You were nothing like what I expected and everything I wanted. We have so much in common and I opened up to you, but you hurt me."

"I'm sorry—"

"That said, I'm in love with you too."

Her smile is radiant as she stands and holds out her hands to me. I grasp them in a daze, and she pulls me to my feet, our bodies so close I can feel the heat radiating off her.

"But you know this is going to be tough, yeah? Enemies to lovers have to work even harder for their happily ever after?"

"Screw the tropes," I growl, hauling her into my arms and hugging her tight. "We're both damn good writers. We can come up with the best fairytale ending ever."

Epilogue

MIA

It's been three long weeks since I've seen Axel and I'm so hyper I'm practically bouncing in the passenger seat of Cole's pickup.

"Tell me again why Axel couldn't get me from the station?"

Cole grunts. He hasn't said much on my previous visits and is inclined to say even less today for some reason. He's protecting his boss. Those two are up to something. I can feel it.

"Does he have a surprise for me?"

Cole doesn't take his eyes off the road, but I sense an eye roll. "Don't you have a book to read?"

"Why, when bugging you is much more fun?"

He snickers. "Well, quit it. I'm not in the mood."

"Wow. When I arrive at the house, I better warn Mr. Darcy you're in a foul mood so he needs to steer clear in case you kick him."

He gives me side eye. "I would never harm that cat."

"I know. Just messing with you."

His sigh is heartfelt, like he has the weight of the world on his shoulders, and at complete odds with the guy who's got a heart of gold.

Since Axel and I got together, I've visited twice, for long weekends. Cole has picked me up both times and while he's reserved, he's usually a little chattier than this. Something's definitely up but I won't bug him. We're almost at the house and I'm bursting out of my skin.

Because this visit, I get to stay for a month.

A blissful thirty days with the guy I love.

Seven hundred and twenty glorious hours we'll spend brainstorming and writing and 'researching' his erotica scenes firsthand. Turns out, that old cliché about absence making the heart grow fonder is true, and our reunions are scorching.

I can't believe this is happening, how much my life has changed since I let down my guard and allowed Axel into my life. I've gone part-time at the newspaper, which gives me more time to write. I'm neck-deep in revisions Christine sent me and I want to make my story shine for when she pitches it to publishers. And having the best critique partner in the business helps too, though Axel tends to distract me, in the best possible way.

We have a plan. We're splitting our time between Manhattan and Sugar Plain. When we're in the writing zone, we'll hide away at his place. When he's doing promotional stuff—and running critique classes for budding writers, a new direction for him which I think is fabulous as he's so good at it —he'll be in the city. Win-win.

As we pull into the drive, I see Axel open the front door and my heart swells. He's waiting for me.

I let out an excited squeal and hear Cole mutter, "Seriously?"

I chuckle and Cole barely stops the pickup before I'm flinging open the door and tumbling out of it.

Axel's elated expression matches mine as he runs toward me, and we meet halfway. An alpha hero who's unafraid of showing his beta core. I love it. My very own cinnamon roll hero.

"Hey, gorgeous." He kisses me like we've spent three months apart rather than three weeks and I clutch at him, never wanting to let go. Excitement fizzes in my veins, tempered by a calmness that this man never fails to elicit when I'm around him.

That special feeling of coming home.

"I've missed you," I whisper against the side of his mouth, wrapping my arms around him.

"Ditto." He sweeps my hair back from my face and stares at me like he's trying to drink in every inch. "I have a surprise for you."

"I knew it." I playfully whack him on the arm. "I tried to grill Cole, but he wouldn't say much."

"He's a good man."

"The best," Cole says as he traipses toward us. "And also the dumbest, for being roped into your schemes."

My eyebrows rise. "Schemes?"

Cole shakes his head as he heads toward the back of the house while Axel snags my hand. "Come inside and I'll show you."

I practically skip up the steps and through the front door, almost tripping over Mr. Darcy in the process. He's sitting on a small round rug I haven't seen before in the middle of the hallway.

"Hey, mister." I squat to scratch him behind the ears, the low rumble he emits indicating he's missed me too. "Never thought I'd admit this, but I think I'm starting to like you."

He rubs his head against my hand and Axel squats too, stroking him from head to tail.

"He's got under my skin a little too." He points at the rug. "The last two times you've left he's sat in this same spot staring at the door, emitting the loudest heart-rending meows, so I got him this rug to keep him warm while he pines."

"Aww, that's so sweet." After a final tickle under the chin for Mr. Darcy, we stand, and I can't tear my eyes off this complex man with a heart of gold. "Now where's my surprise?"

"In here." He opens the library door and I murmur, "I've already seen the surprises you spring on me in here."

Our gaze lock and the amber flecks in his eyes smolder as we remember our first time in this room and how our tumultuous relationship snowballed from there.

"I intend on locking this door later, but for now..." When we reach the desk, he spins his computer screen around and I see Rosie beaming at me.

"Hey girlfriend," she yells, waving madly at me. "Long time no see."

"We had drinks last night." Confused, I glance at Axel, and he murmurs, "I'll leave you two to chat."

He leaves the library and I sit in his chair, pulling the screen closer. "You're the surprise? But what I want to know is, why you didn't call me instead of Axel?"

Rosie's smug as she sits back. "That's because your delicious man and I had business to discuss."

She's aiming for blasé, but I know my friend and she's fidgeting like crazy, shifting her weight side to side on the chair.

"Business?"

She nods. "You're looking at Adele Lavash's new publicist."

I gape a little and she screams so loudly I jump. "Can you

believe it? Me, representing Axel's alter ego?" She does a little shimmy and I laugh, beyond thrilled for her.

"That's great news. I'm happy for you."

"That's not the best part." Rosie leans forward like she's about to impart a secret. "I'm coming to visit!"

"You're coming *here*?"

Rosie setting foot out of Manhattan is on par with her flying to the moon.

"Yeah, can you believe it? I need to spend some one-on-one time with Axel so I can formulate a plan for how we launch him properly and with you there for a while, now seemed to be the best time." She waggles her finger at me. "But don't worry, I'm giving you a week of obscene catching up before I arrive."

We laugh and I can't believe my best friend will be staying with us. "It's going to be great. Wait until you see Sugar Plain. It's Stars Hollow on steroids."

"Yay." She claps her hands like a little kid. "By the way, who's the fine lumberjack of a man I glimpsed behind Axel when we talked online the other day?"

"You mean Cole?"

"Cole..." She tries the name on for size and I stifle a laugh at the thought of bona fide city girl Rosie making a play for country boy Cole. They're a huge mismatch. Then again, look at Axel and me.

I'd love to see Rosie find a great guy, but the taciturn Cole isn't it. It's two broken hearts waiting to happen.

"Anyway, I have to run." She grimaces. "I have to break up with Jace."

"Technically, you have to be dating to break up and I thought you haven't seen him for two weeks?"

"Yeah, but he wants to go away to Bear Mountain for the weekend and that's not going to happen, so best I make a clean break." She makes a slicing motion like she's wielding a sword. "I'll call you in a few days, okay? After you do lots of this with that dreamy guy of yours." She makes smooching sounds and I laugh as she disconnects.

Relieved she didn't get her heart broken by Jace and thrilled she's coming here, I go in search of Axel. He's in the living room, standing by the fireplace, reading the blurb on the back of a book. His brow is furrowed as he concentrates, and I'm overcome by how familiar each and every one of his expressions are to me now.

The soft cotton of his oldest T shirt clings to his chest and the grey sweatpants he favors when writing sculpt his long legs, and while I'd like nothing better to divest him of those clothes, I need a moment to savor our reunion.

"Hey," I say softly, and he glances up from the book, his frown instantly clearing as he puts it down. "Any good?"

"It's an ARC Chrissie sent me, a debut mystery author who needs all the quotes she can get. Haven't started it yet, but the blurb has me hooked."

"I wonder if you'll get to do that for me one day." I cross the living room and step into his arms. "Maybe even give me an Axel Low cover quote?" I bat my eyelashes at him. "I'll be eternally grateful."

He chuckles and, with his chest pressed against mine, I feel it all the way down to my toes. "That sounds awfully like bribery to me."

"Call it an incentive." I nip the tender skin under his jaw, and he groans. "One of many."

His hands skim my back, drifting upward to rest on my shoulders momentarily, before cupping my face. "Considering how much I love you, I'll do anything."

"In that case, a brilliant cover quote and a rousing endorsement on national television?"

He doesn't remind me I haven't finished edits on my

manuscript let alone sold it. Axel has my back. Now and always. How did I get so lucky?

"Deal." He kisses me to seal it. "How did you like your surprise?"

"It's fantastic." I hesitate, reluctant to ask the one question that's been bugging me since Rosie told me the news. "Rosie's great, but you're not just hiring her because she's my best friend, are you?"

He shakes his head. "I researched PR firms thoroughly and I like what she brings to the table. Her enthusiasm is second to none and her being your bestie is a bonus."

"Great." I tap my bottom lip, pretending to think. "How can I ever repay you?"

His grin is positively wicked. "I have a few ideas..."

As we hold hands and head up the hallway toward the bedroom, Mr. Darcy lets out a particularly loud purr of approval.

🐈

For an exclusive bonus epilogue from Mr. Darcy's point of view, sign up here.

I hope you enjoyed **DID NOT FINISH**. As Axel and Mia know, every review counts, so please consider leaving one for this book.

For bookish fun, join the Nicola Marsh Reader Room on Facebook.

ONE STAR REVIEW

Rosie and Cole's story

Coming in 2024

ROSIE: I'm a bonafide city girl. I don't leave Manhattan. Ever. But when bestselling author Axel Low wants to embrace indie publishing and launch his new pseudonym, I can't pass up the opportunity. My one-woman PR company is struggling, so I travel to the wilds of Nebraska to boost my career.

I need this job. I don't need some big, burly lumberjack who thinks he knows best telling me what to do.

COLE: Rosie is a menace. She should head back to the city where she belongs. She's not qualified to boost my best friend's career. There are no billboards in Sugar Plain and her digital plans to go viral are questionable.

It doesn't helps that she drives me crazy and I want her more than I've ever wanted anything. A few one star reviews online should get her scurrying back to the city.

Until we're stuck together during a road trip and all bets are off...

If you enjoyed DID NOT FINISH, you'll love FAKING IT.

⯪⯪ ⯪⯪⯪ **"Should be at the top of everyone's 'must read' list. It's that good. Please treat yourself to this terrific novel by the talented Nicola Marsh."**Susan Wiggs, NYT bestselling author.

I need to get a life. Preferably someone else's.

Single, homeless and jobless, I agree to my best friend's whacky scheme: travel to Mumbai, pose as Amrita, my Indian BFF, and ditch the fiancé her traditional Indian parents have chosen.

Simple.

Until I'm mistaken for a famous Bollywood actress, stalked by a cowboy wannabe, courted by an English lord, and busted by the blackmailing fiancé.

Life is less complicated in New York. Or so I think, until the entourage of crazies follow me to the Big Apple and that's when the fun really begins.

I deal with a blossoming romance, an addiction to Indian food and my first movie role, while secretly craving another trip to the mystical land responsible for sparking my new lease on life. Returning to my Indian birthplace, I have an epiphany.

Maybe the happily-ever-after of my dreams isn't so far away?

Acknowledgments

This story has been sheer fun to write from start to finish.

It started as a glimmer of an idea because I'm always grateful to anyone who takes the time to read and review my books.

The reading community is vast, and don't get me started on BookTok. My to-be-read pile has grown exponentially with every video I watch!

But I love reading. I'm a reader at heart. The writing flowed on from there.

So I'd like to give a HUGE shoutout to all the readers, reviewers, bookstagrammers, booktokers, librarians, booksellers and fellow bookworms who read and review. Without you, this book wouldn't have been written.

Thanks to Karen, Grace, Pamela, Tess, Amy, Christine and Susan, for your generosity in sharing publishing knowledge. Hoping to meet you all in person one day and give you squishy hugs.

Thank to MaryAnn, who's always a DM away and is so willing to help. I appreciate you so much!

To Suz Grimwood Graphic Design for the cover.

To the members of my Readers Room on Facebook, I love interacting with you all and the ideas you spark, like the setting for this story.

My writing buddies, Soraya and Natalie, who are always there for me.

My folks, who support me through it all.

My beautiful boys, this one's for you too, as always.

Martin, who listens to me lament the occasional DNF. (Don't you love how subjective reading is?)

Last but not least, for all of you who love books as much as I do. I hope this story brings a smile to you face.

FREE book and more

SIGN UP TO NICOLA'S NEWSLETTER for a free book!

Read Nicola's feel-good romance **DID NOT FINISH**

Or her gothic suspense novels **THE RETREAT** and **THE HAVEN**

Try the **CARTWRIGHT BROTHERS** duo

FASCINATION

PERFECTION

The **WORKPLACE LIAISONS** duo

THE BOSS

THE CEO

Try the **BASHFUL BRIDES** series

NOT THE MARRYING KIND

NOT THE ROMANTIC KIND

NOT THE DARING KIND

NOT THE DATING KIND

The **CREATIVE IN LOVE** series

THE GRUMPY GUY

THE SHY GUY

THE GOOD GUY

Try the **BOMBSHELLS** series

BEFORE (FREE!)

BRASH

BLUSH

BOLD

BAD

BOMBSHELLS BOXED SET

The **WORLD APART** series

WALKING THE LINE (FREE!)

CROSSING THE LINE

TOWING THE LINE

BLURRING THE LINE

WORLD APART BOXED SET

The **HOT ISLAND NIGHTS** duo

WICKED NIGHTS

WANTON NIGHTS

The **BOLLYWOOD BILLIONAIRES** series

FAKING IT

MAKING IT

The **LOOKING FOR LOVE** series

LUCKY LOVE

CRAZY LOVE

SAPPHIRES ARE A GUY'S BEST FRIEND

THE SECOND CHANCE GUY

Check out Nicola's website for a full list of her books.

And read her other romances as Nikki North.

'MILLIONAIRE IN THE CITY' series.

LUCKY

COCKY

CRAZY

FANCY

FLIRTY

FOLLY

MADLY

Check out the **ESCAPE WITH ME** series.

DATE ME

LOVE ME

DARE ME

TRUST ME

FORGIVE ME

Try the **LAW BREAKER** series

THE DEAL MAKER
THE CONTRACT BREAKER

About the Author

USA TODAY bestselling and multi-award winning author Nicola Marsh writes page-turning fiction to keep you up all night.

She's published 82 books and sold 8 million copies worldwide. She currently writes contemporary romance and domestic suspense.

She's also a Waldenbooks, Bookscan, Amazon, iBooks and Barnes & Noble bestseller, a RBY (Romantic Book of the Year) and National Readers' Choice Award winner, and a multi-finalist for a number of awards including the Romantic Times Reviewers' Choice Award, HOLT Medallion, Booksellers' Best, Golden Quill, Laurel Wreath, and More than Magic.

A physiotherapist for thirteen years, she now adores writing full time, raising her two dashing young heroes, sharing fine food with family and friends, and her favorite, curling up with a good book!

www.ingramcontent.com/pod-product-compliance
Lightning Source LLC
Chambersburg PA
CBHW031259120726
47906CB00003B/810